REVENGE

OF THE ANGELS

REVENGE
OF THE ANGELS

JENNIFER ZIEGLER

SCHOLASTIC PRESS / NEW YORK

• Library of Congress Cataloging-in-Publication Data • Ziegler, Jennifer, 1967- author. • Revenge of the angels / Jennifer Ziegler. — First edition. • pages cm • Summary: The eleven-year-old Brewster triplets, Dawn, Darby, and Delaney, are afraid this is going to be the worst Christmas ever — they have been cast as angels in their local Christmas pageant just because they are girls, their mother, older sister, and aunt are stuck in Boston because of the snow, someone is stealing outdoor Christmas decorations and baked goods, and their father is just too busy for Christmas. • ISBN 978-0-545-83899-3 (hardcover) — ISBN 978-0-545-83958-7 (ebook) 1. Triplets — Juvenile fiction. 2. Sisters — Juvenile fiction. 3. Divorced parents — Juvenile fiction. 4. Families — Texas — Juvenile fiction. 5. Christmas stories. 6. Texas — Juvenile fiction. [1. Triplets — Fiction. 2. Sisters — Fiction. 3. Divorce — Fiction. 4. Family life — Texas — Fiction. 5. Christmas — Fiction. 6. Humorous stories. 7. Texas — Fiction.] I. Title. • PZ7.Z4945Re 2015 • 813.6 — dc23 • [Fic] • 2015007041 • 10 9 8 7 6 5 4 3 2 1   15 16 17 18 19 • Printed in the U.S.A   23 •
First edition, September 2015 • Book design by Yaffa Jaskoll

FOR CLARE DUNKLE —
THANK YOU FOR SHARING YOUR
WISDOM, YOUR STORIES, AND
YOUR GINGERBREAD.

CHAPTER ONE

Peaceful Protest

Delaney

I still say it was Dawn's fault that Christmas was almost ruined. She let that silly pageant take over everything.

Once she has her mind set on how things should be, she's as flexible as a mule in cement shoes. But she also has a way of getting all of us worked up, and before we know it, the three of us are stuck in a situation we can't get out of. Like quicksand.

After the horror of the Christmas pageant auditions and casting announcements, Dawn pouted all the way home and grumped all the way up the stairs to our room. As soon as we shut the door she started griping loudly.

"Angels! Can you believe that? Angels! Do I look like an angel to you?"

Darby and I shook our heads. When Dawn's angry, she can be kind of scary, so we always just agree with her. And truthfully, she didn't look all that angelic with her glaring eyes and all the crisscrossed lines on her brow. Even her hair looked redder.

"This whole thing is such a . . . a . . ." Dawn snapped her fingers, trying to think of the right word.

"A travesty," Darby said.

"A catastrophe," I said.

"More like an epic disgrace," Dawn said. "Those auditions were a total sham!"

We'd practiced long and hard to be the Three Wise Men at our church's annual pageant. Just that morning, we'd gotten up at the crack of dawn to practice our wise walk, which is not easy. At first we couldn't agree on what a wise walk looked like. We tried gliding, trudging, and marching. Darby even pointed out that in "The First Noel" a line goes, "Then entered in the wise men three, full reverently upon their knee," so we tried walking on our knees. But that hurt our knee-caps, and a harmful knee-walk doesn't seem, or look, very wise.

Finally we found the right walk — a slow tramp with our heads held up high so we could follow the big star and look noble. We'd thought of everything, and we were the wisest-looking of all at the auditions, but instead we were cast as angels.

When we asked Mrs. Higginbotham if we did a good job, she said yes. We said, "But we didn't get to be Wise Men," and she said, "Of course not. Those roles are for boys."

And that was that. Until now.

"It's not right that Lucas, Adam, and Tommy get the parts just because they're boys," Darby said.

"Yeah, I mean, what century does she think she's in? Girls can be anything boys can be. Besides, the baby Jesus is actually a Baby Betsy doll," I said. "If she can be a he, why can't we?"

"Because Mrs. Higginbotham is not being fair," Dawn grumbled. She crossed her arms over her chest and plopped down on her bed.

I plopped down on my bed, too, but kept plopping. The next thing I knew, I was on my feet, jumping on the mattress. It felt good to get the nervousness out — until I accidentally bounced into the shelf between my bed and Dawn's. Books and cards and dominos tumbled everywhere.

"Doggone it, Delaney!" Dawn fussed at me.

I hopped off the bed and started picking up the stuff on the floor. Darby gathered dominos. "I'm sorry. I can't help it. I get jittery whenever I'm mad. Or nervous. Or excited."

"Or awake," Dawn growled.

"I can't help it," I said again. I know I can be annoying with all my bouncing and bustling. I'm the most restless and energetic of my sisters. Dawn says I was born with coffee in my veins. And Darby says I move at a different speed than everyone else. All I know is, I have to move when I'm thinking or feeling stuff. And I guess I'm always thinking or feeling something.

I'm getting better at controlling it, though. This past summer I was even able to stay quiet and sneak up on my sister Lily to make sure she was all right when the Almost Wedding stuff started going crazy. I was really surprised and proud when I did it.

"It's all right," Dawn said to me. She picked up a couple of books close to her feet and put them back on the shelf. "You get jittery when you're upset and I get surly."

"And I feel like curling up and hiding," Darby said. She put the last book back on the shelf and sat down on the floor, pulling her knees to her chest. "I just can't believe we didn't get the part. We worked so hard!"

"Yeah!" I said. I was hopping again — but just on my toes, making sure I stayed in one spot. "Now that we're angels, we won't get to do our wise walk! We don't even get to walk. We just stand there and sway and pretend like we're flying."

"Oh, well. At least you might be better at swaying than doing the wise walk. You were always too speedy," Darby said to me. She's always trying to look on the bright side.

"You make a pretty good angel, Darby," I told her. It was true. She had a peaceful-happy look on her face while we were auditioning. "You'll be great at it."

"What are you two doing?" Dawn hollered. "Why are you talking like we're going along with this whole debacle? We aren't!"

Darby and I knew what would happen next.

Sure enough, Dawn called out, "Meeting in the Triangular Office! Now!" Only we were already in the Triangular Office. Our bedroom is in the attic, so the ceiling is pitched like the roof. And the floor, of course, is flat, making a triangular shape.

Dawn pounded her headboard with her fist, as if it were a gavel, to call the meeting to order. Dawn runs the meetings because she is the oldest triplet —

and the bossiest. Besides, she plans to be president when she grows up. I'm going to be Speaker of the House and Darby is going to be chief justice. Those are both important jobs, but the president is the head of government, so we let her summon us out of respect for the office.

"Darby, you take notes," Dawn directed. "Let's list everything that led up to this calamity."

Darby sat in front of the computer on our big desk and we stood behind her, Dawn at her left shoulder and me at her right. Then we all took turns dictating what had happened.

This is what Darby typed:

This morning, Mom dropped us off at church approximately forty-five minutes early in order to audition for the annual Christmas Eve Pageant. We were trying out for the part of the Three Wise Men.

Mom didn't stick around because she had lots of packing to do. She and Lily are going to Boston to see Aunt Jane. This bothers us because Lily just got home from college. Also, we want to see Aunt Jane, too. But that doesn't have anything to do with our audition.

Let the record state that the three of us had spent

three full days practicing. We knew that if you want to win a part at an audition, you have to be the best at it. That meant we had to be the wisest-looking of all the other kids. The way you look wise is to make your face look not happy or sad, so no frowning or smiling. But you can't look like a robot, either. You have to look like you are thinking about something really important all the time.

Mr. and Mrs. Higginbotham were in charge of the auditions. They are the bosses of the church. We don't remember there being an election, but Mrs. Higginbotham tells people what to do all the time.

Three boys from our middle school group were also there: Lucas Westbrook, who lives down the road from us, and his pals Adam and Tommy Ybarra. Plus, there were a few kids we didn't know who were younger than us. Also there were Lucy Beasley and Wilson Cantu, who are in eighth grade and are boyfriend and girlfriend. They had already told everyone that they wanted to be Mary and Joseph. Everyone was fine with that.

Mr. Higginbotham worked the sounds and lights while Mrs. Higginbotham supervised the tryouts. Of all the people who auditioned for the Wise Men, we were the best by far. Here is the evidence:

Lucas's cowboy boots made such a loud *clomp-clomp* that the little kids put their hands over their ears.

Adam was really slow and kept rolling his eyes.

Tommy kept saying "Frankenstein" instead of "frankincense."

And all the little kids who tried out as Wise Men had a real hard time standing still. Even Delaney managed not to bounce around, which proves we were super prepared.

No one else tried to look smart and regal. No one else made big round eyes to show they were beholding something wondrous. They just walked their regular walks and looked their regular looks. But when Mrs. Higginbotham announced the cast list, she said Lucas, Adam, and Tommy would be the Wise Men. We would be angels.

Then Mom picked us up. She told Mrs. Higginbotham it was really nice of her to head up auditions with all the other things she was doing for the church. Mrs. Higginbotham said she doesn't do it for personal glory, she helps out because she is a good person.

She then told Mom to bring cookies for the pageant reception.

Mom said she'd planned to bring a cobbler.

Mrs. Higginbotham told her the Murchisons were already bringing cobbler and we can't have too much of one thing. Then she walked away.

On the way home, we told Mom we liked her cobbler and that it was the best dessert she made. Also, we reminded her that you can't have too much of a good thing. It's what Dad said when we were born.

Mom told us she'd rather make cookies than make a fuss.

Dawn made a grunting noise as Darby typed and said, "I'd rather make a fuss."

Darby stopped typing. "I think that's everything," she said.

"So . . . what do we do now?" I asked.

"First off," Dawn said, "I think we need to stop referring to the roles as 'Wise Men' and call them 'Wise People' instead. That way maybe we can convince everyone that girls can do the parts, too."

"Agreed," Darby said.

"Agreed," I said.

"Secondly," Dawn continued, "we need to change the Higginbothams' minds. We need to show them that we are not angels — we're Wise People."

"Agreed," Darby said.

"Agreed," I said.

It was quiet for a moment. Then I said, "So how are we going to do that?"

None of us had any ideas.

We sat and sat and thought and thought and then, when no one said anything, moped and moped. After a long while, Darby, in a real quiet voice, said, "Maybe we could . . . call her?"

"Call who?" Dawn asked.

"Mrs. Higginbotham," Darby answered. "Maybe if we just explained how we feel, she'll realize she made the wrong decision?"

Dawn tapped her finger against her chin. "I suppose we don't have anything to lose by trying."

We voted on the proposed solution, and it passed. We then decided we needed to be very clear about what we wanted to say, so we worked out a speech. Everyone took turns talking while Darby typed, and then we all edited. If we disagreed, Darby arbitrated, and Dawn got final veto power. Eventually, we were done. After we printed it, we went downstairs to Mom's office. Mom was back in her room packing, so we were pretty sure we'd have privacy.

Dawn was still in too sour a mood to be polite on the phone and Darby was too shy, so I was the triplet to make the call. When you're a triplet, you have to be prepared to step in and take action whenever your siblings are overly crabby or chicken or anything like that. It's a fair trade, since they'll do things for me that require being still. Also, it felt good to know they had faith in me. Of course, they made me promise to stick to our speech and put the call on speakerphone so that they could hear.

I looked up the Higginbothams in the church directory on Mom's desk, punched the number into the phone, and swallowed hard. My left foot jiggled eight times with each ring. Finally, a familiar voice answered.

"Higginbotham residence. Lois Higginbotham speaking."

"Hello, Mrs. Higginbotham. This is Delaney Brewster. How are you?" My foot was still jiggling, making my voice shake a little.

"I'm fine, Delaney." She sounded surprised. "To what do I owe this courtesy?"

"Um . . . You don't owe anything. I'm just calling to talk."

"Yes. Why are you calling me at home, Delaney? Is something wrong?"

"No. Well . . . yes. Kinda. I mean . . ." Darby and Dawn could tell I was about to start rambling all over the place, so they started jabbing their fingers toward our prepared script. I cleared my throat. "You see, Mrs. Higginbotham, I was calling about the casting decisions for the pageant."

"Yes?"

"I truly believe my sisters and I did a good job at the audition. We practiced hard and I know I walked a little too fast, but I can keep on practicing that, and if my face gets twitchy I can always tie a bandana —"

Dawn shoved the paper in my face and made mad eyes at me. Darby made begging motions with her hands.

"The three of you were marvelous," Mrs. Higginbotham said. "You did a great job and you'll be beautiful angels. Is that all?"

"No. It's just . . . We didn't want to be angels. We wanted to be the Three Wise Men." Again Dawn waved the script in front of me and stomped her foot. "I mean, the Three Wise People."

"I see."

"So, um . . . is there any chance that you might reconsider your casting decisions?"

There was a noise like wind as she sighed into the phone. "I'm afraid I can't do that, Delaney. If I give you three the parts, I would be disappointing three new people. Those boys wanted to be in the pageant, too, let's not forget. And that's not fair to them, is it?"

"Um . . ." I didn't know what to say. I looked over at Dawn and Darby to see what they thought. Darby was nodding slowly and sadly, as if she agreed, but Dawn was shaking her head and frowning.

But Mrs. Higginbotham didn't wait for me to answer. "It's just not possible for me to make changes at this point," she said. "I'm sure you understand."

"I . . . suppose I do?" I wasn't sure what to say. I had no idea how I felt and wasn't sure how to speak for all of us. But it seemed like I had no choice. Mrs. Higginbotham made it seem like I had to say I understood — even though I didn't.

"You three will be marvelous angels."

"Thanks?"

"Yes. Oh! And tell your mother to bring sugar cookies. Someone else is bringing chocolate chip. Bye now!"

"What a waste of time," Dawn grumbled after I hung up.

"She sort of had a point," Darby said. "If she tries to make us happy, she'll just make others unhappy. It's a no-win situation."

"I guess there's nothing we can do," I said.

"But . . . but . . ." Dawn's face looked mad and helpless at the same time. She moved her mouth as if she was going to say something, then suddenly gave up, made a growling noise, and marched back upstairs.

Dawn doesn't like losing. None of us do, but especially Dawn. I knew it wasn't just the fact that we didn't get the parts we wanted that bothered her. It was that it hadn't been a fair fight. We can't help it if we're girls instead of boys.

It looked like we were stuck being swaying, frowning, overruled angels instead of Wise People. Just like Mom would be making cookies instead of cobbler. And we were getting cheated out of a few days with Lily. And we wouldn't get to see Aunt Jane.

So far, this was not shaping up to be a very merry Christmas.

CHAPTER TWO

Riders

Dawn

Mynah birds are tropical, and even though we are in a temperate zone, Central Texas is warm and humid, so it will feel like home to him — or her. Also, they are gregarious, which means they like to be with other creatures, so I can hang out with him — or her — all the time, which will make him — or her — happier. And that's why I want a pet anyway, because I like to be social, too, and when I talk to Quincy, he mainly just falls asleep and —"

"Jiminy, Delaney, do you breathe through your ears?" I said. I just couldn't take her jabbering anymore.

Mom turned around from one of the van's middle seats and raised an eyebrow at me. "Dawn, be nice."

Then she turned to Delaney, who was sitting in the bucket seat beside her. "Delaney, let's let other people talk for a while, okay?"

"Fine," she said in a morose voice. "I was just answering Alex's question."

When we pulled onto the highway leaving Johnson City toward Austin, Alex, who was driving, had looked at us in the rearview mirror and asked what we all wanted for Christmas. Thirty minutes and one whole town later, Delaney was still talking about that dang mynah bird she wanted.

"It's okay, Delaney," Alex said. "I appreciate your telling me about the birds. I learned a lot."

Lily, who was sitting beside him in the front passenger seat, smiled at him. He noticed and smiled back. They do that a lot, and it's like there are sparkles in the air between them.

Except for a span of about eight months last year, Lily and Alex have been girlfriend and boyfriend since high school, so Alex is part of our family and we love him almost as much as we love Lily. When they were broken up, Lily seemed to be . . . well . . . broken. Her forehead always had squiggly lines in it, and she was all listless and droopy. Now that they're together again, she's back to being herself — smiling and shining and perky.

Sometimes we'll see Lily staring at Alex when he doesn't know it — or Alex staring at Lily when she doesn't know it — and they get these quiet-happy expressions on their faces. I don't know how they're feeling on the inside, but from the outside it looks cozy and relaxed.

"So who's next?" Lily asked, turning in her seat to face us. "What other presents are you asking for?"

"All I want for Christmas is a zip line," Darby said.

"A zip line!" Alex repeated, sounding amused. None of us were surprised.

Darby is an enormous contradiction, because even though she's super shy around people, she is the bravest one when it comes to haunted houses, jumps off the high dive, or bicycle stunts. Plus, she often thinks up harebrained daredevil schemes of her own — a few of which haven't turned out all that well.

"A zip line is crazy," I pointed out. "You'll crack your head open."

She shook her head. "I'll wear a helmet."

"You could still fracture ribs or break bones," Delaney said. "Or maybe land on a rattlesnake or a fire ant mound and get bitten, which could make you swell up and turn colors and —"

"Enough!" Mom ordered while holding up her hands in surrender. She does that a lot, and we know better than to push when she does.

"What about you, Dawn?" Alex asked.

I sat up straight and cleared my throat. I knew I could make a stronger argument for my Christmas present than any of the others. For weeks I'd been pondering this, and I had lots of good points to back me up. "If I had my own megaphone, I could alert everyone with important announcements. I could also warn neighbors of any impending threats, and it would help me reach a bigger audience when I give speeches."

"But what if we don't want to hear your speeches?" Darby said.

"Excuse me?" I said. "That's a rude thing to say."

Darby hunched her shoulders. "What I mean is . . . What if other important things are going on during your speech, but we don't know about them because you're being so loud and stuff?"

"Yeah," Delaney said. "Besides, you can't run for president until you're thirty-five years old."

"I can do plenty until then." I held my head high. "All I'm saying is that my gift isn't a toy or a pet — it's a tool that will allow me to help my community and fulfill my civic duty."

I saw Darby and Delaney exchange eye-rolly glances. I didn't care, though. They were just jealous that they didn't make as strong a case for their gifts.

"Girls, I hate to keep disappointing you," Mom said in a tired-sounding voice, "but I'm not going to get those gifts."

"You mean the raucous mynah bird and the very dangerous zip line, right?" I asked.

"I mean all of them," Mom said. "We can't take in unpredictable exotic pets. I can't afford any more trips to the emergency room. And with my headaches and our neighbor's penchant for calling the police anytime she's startled, a megaphone is out of the question. I'm sorry, but that's how it is."

Darby, Delaney, and I looked helplessly at each other. I started to open my mouth, but Darby put her hand on my arm and shook her head. It was a reminder. I'm really good at convincing most people, but arguing with Mom only makes things worse.

We moped the rest of the way to Austin. It wasn't fair.

It wasn't like we were handing over a list of fifty-seven expensive toys, games, and gadgets like spoiled Lucas Westbrook does every Christmas (he gets everything on it). We were each asking for one item. One *reasonable* item.

Twenty minutes later, we were driving up to the airport. Alex pulled up the van alongside a big sidewalk. People with suitcases were hurrying in and out of the automatic glass doors in front of the terminal. There was lots of noise and lots of action and it seemed like everything was going faster than normal.

We all climbed out of the van to hug Mom and Lily good-bye.

"Tell Aunt Jane we miss her and we don't think it's fair that we don't get to see her and that she needs to come visit again soon," Delaney said.

"Be careful," Darby said. She sounded a little sniffly.

"You'll call us, right?" I asked. Mom and Lily assured me they would.

Lily stepped over to Alex and they smooched on the lips.

When we were little we used to bunch up our faces and say "Ew!" or "Yuck!" whenever we saw them kiss. Later, when we were older, we would go "Aww!" all together in a chorus, which would embarrass them. Now we just grin at each other and stay quiet. It's like we're too scared to do anything that might break the spell. We don't want them to ever break up again. So to give them their privacy, Darby, Delaney, and I got back into the van, with me taking the seat Mom had been in.

Lily and Alex pulled apart and stepped backward slowly until just their hands were holding. Then they let go. Alex climbed in the car and the four of us watched as Mom and Lily stepped through the glass doors and disappeared into the crowd inside the airport.

All four of us wore glum faces as we headed back toward Johnson City.

"It's not fair," Darby said from the back. "Lily just got here and now she's leaving."

"Yeah! She only gets a couple of weeks off before she has to go back to school and we're getting cheated out of four of those days!" Delaney said.

"It's a real hornswoggle, all right," I said. I waited for Alex to say something in agreement. After a moment of quiet, I asked, "Aren't you upset, too, Alex?"

Our eyes met in the rearview mirror. "No," he said. "I mean, I'll miss her, but I'm not upset. Have you three noticed how excited she is about graduate school?"

We nodded. Lily is thinking about studying library science, which sounds like a place where people wear lab coats and do experiments on books, but it's not. Lily said it's where you learn how to help people find information, anything from books to magazines to recordings to films — whatever people might need for their studies or work or just to enjoy. It does sound like the perfect job for Lily.

"But don't you love her? Don't you want to spend time with her?" Delaney said.

"Of course I love her," Alex said. "When you love someone, you want them to be happy. She's really excited about becoming a librarian, and I want to help her achieve that. So I'm happy that she gets to go look at these schools. Does that make sense?"

We sat quietly, thinking about it.

After a while, Darby said, "I guess it's kind of selfish to want people all to yourself, even if you love them."

Delaney and I turned around to look at her, confused.

"Think about it," she went on. "We don't mind when Lily spends time with Alex away from us, because we see that he makes her happy. This is the same thing. Alex sees that becoming a librarian will make Lily happy, so he doesn't mind that she's spending time looking at those schools. Am I right, Alex?"

"You got it," Alex said.

"It still stinks," I muttered, crossing my arms and leaning back in my seat.

We fell silent again. Beside me, Delaney was all fidgety. I glanced out at the passing scenery.

Normally, I'm so excited this time of year that I bounce almost as much as Delaney. I love Christmas. It's when Lily comes home, decorations are everywhere, Mom's house smells like whatever we've been baking, Dad constantly plays Christmas songs at his apartment, and Aunt Jane visits. But this year everything is all topsy-turvy because of Mom and Lily's trip, with Aunt Jane not coming because she visited in June for the Almost Wedding, Dad working extra, and that confounded pageant. It didn't feel all that merry yet.

Alex must have been thinking the same thing because he suddenly said, "Let's all cheer up. It's Christmas! Tell me . . . have you all finished your shopping yet?"

The three of us groaned.

"Whoops. Sorry," Alex said. "Did I bring up a sore subject?"

"It's okay. We just have an impossible job," Darby said.

"What's so impossible about it?" he asked.

"Mom," I replied. "She's impossible to buy gifts for."

"It's true," Delaney said. "Dad's easy. He loves gadgets or joke stuff, and we can always find those. And Lily is easy, because she likes so many things — pretty boxes or homemade bracelets or calendars with sunset photos or those natural soaps at the farmers' market that smell like berries or —"

"He knows!" I said.

"Anyway," Delaney went on, making her annoyed face at me, "Mom is really tough. She's picky about what she likes."

"What sorts of things does she ask for or say that she wants?" Alex asked.

"Peace and quiet," Delaney said.

"Order," Darby said.

"A trip to Europe," I said, remembering how she said that once.

"I see your dilemma," Alex said. "But you three will figure something out. You are just about the smartest people I know. And when the three of you put your heads together, there's pretty much nothing you can't do."

Darby, Delaney, and I looked at each other and smiled. It felt good to have Alex believe in us.

"Just, um . . . don't overdo things, okay? The town is still recovering from the last time you all strategized." He was grinning, but his eyes had a worried look. "Tell you what," Alex said, looking at us in the rearview mirror. "Let's not talk about anything. Let's just play Presidential Trivia."

We all shouted, "Hooray!"

Presidential Trivia is probably our favorite pastime, but for some strange reason, not many people will play it with us. Usually Alex asks us questions, but today we took turns asking him questions.

First, Delaney asked, "Which president worked for a while as a stand-up comedian before getting elected?" and Alex already knew it was Ronald Reagan.

Then Darby asked, "Which president had a pet bear, badger, and hyena while he lived in the White House?" and Alex correctly guessed Teddy Roosevelt.

That left me to try to stump him. "Okay," I said, sitting forward. "Which president lost the White House china in a card game?"

"Wow. Um . . . Let me see . . ." Alex considered for a moment. When he thinks hard he lowers his brow and tilts his head from side to side — as if trying to make the right answer roll out of a hiding place in his head. "That's a stumper."

"Give up?" I asked.

"Yep."

"Warren G. Harding!" Darby and Delaney said together.

Before I knew it, things started looking familiar and we were pulling into the long gravel drive leading to Mom's house.

Dad was supposed to have already been there, but instead our neighbor, Mr. Neighbor, walked over and said that Dad had called to explain he was running a little late.

"Why don't you come over and have some hot chocolate while you wait?" he asked us.

Alex parked Mom's van under the carport roof and gave me her keys for safekeeping. We waved as he got into his brown car with the Tulane bumper sticker on it — which had been too small to take us all to the airport — and drove away.

I hated having so many good-byes in one day.

You know when you have a splinter stuck in your

finger? You know how it aches? Not the kind where you're screaming or moaning, but that constant twinge reminding you that things aren't right? Well, that was how it felt to see Mom and Lily go through those glass doors and know that they'd be far away for a while — like the start of a small, steady pain.

Knowing we wouldn't get the presents we'd asked for was another splinter. And having to be angels instead of Wise People was another. One splinter might be tolerable. But three?

So as Alex's car disappeared from view, I couldn't help but moan a little. All at once there were too many aches to deal with.

CHAPTER THREE

Wise Counsel

Darby

Mr. and Mrs. Neighbor live across the street from us, and we drop by all the time. In the summer they let us run around in their sprinklers, since we like theirs better than our automatic ones, and they treat us to homemade ice cream — yum! When it's cold, they invite us over for hot chocolate and homemade gingerbread. Visiting the Neighbors is one of our favorite things to do all year long.

Just walking toward their house made my gloomy mood ease up a bit, but I could still feel that squeeze-y sensation in my chest — the one I get when I'm upset or excited or have just eaten a hot pepper. It usually leads to the hiccups. So while Dawn and Delaney followed Mrs.

Neighbor inside to help with the hot chocolate, I hung back, feeling sullen and trying to stop that first loud "*hic!*" from coming out. Plus, I wanted to admire the porch.

The Neighbors have a big wraparound porch, like we do. On ours you'll find a squeaky porch swing, a big smelly dog crate, bicycle helmets, a pogo stick, some broken brooms we use for playing Quidditch, muddy boots that we can't wear inside and are too lazy to clean off, and a rusty watering can that sometimes has a lizard hiding in it.

But the Neighbors' porch is like an outdoor living room. They have lots of white wicker chairs, love seats, benches, and rockers, all with comfy cushions, flowering plants, and a couple of tables that always have something wonderful on them — like a pitcher of lemonade or a checkers game.

Since the start of December their porch has been extra nice, with colored lights all along the roof, red bows and greenery along the rails, and a wreath made of holly, pine cones, and gold-colored ribbon hanging on the door.

"You have the coziest, most Christmas-y house of all," I told Mr. Neighbor.

"Why, thank you," he said. "Want to see my favorite Christmas decoration?" He walked over to one of the tables on the porch and picked up a Santa Claus figurine. It looked old. In fact, it didn't look like any Santa I'd ever seen before. This one wasn't a round, jolly guy in a red suit. Instead, he had a stern expression and was wearing a robe made out of some sort of brown fur with a rope belt. If it weren't for the long white beard and the fact that he was holding a Christmas tree, I wouldn't have known who he was.

"Why is Santa so surly?" I asked.

Mr. Neighbor laughed. "That's good ol' St. Nick," he said. "He's not surly, he's just a little worse for wear. He's been in my family a long time."

"Is he a priceless antique?"

"Well, I don't know about how much he's worth to other folks, but he's priceless to me. I remember seeing him in my grandfather's house over the holidays when I was a boy."

I squinted at him. It was tough to imagine Mr. Neighbor as a little boy, because of his gray hair and crinkled skin and the way his voice sounds all scratchy and bullfrog-y.

"Each Christmas I used to hold this fellow," Mr. Neighbor said, staring down at the Santa in his hands, "and make a wish."

"Did they come true?" I asked.

He glanced upward and rubbed the whiskers on his chin, lost in thought. "Well . . . some of my wishes came true. I don't know if St. Nick did it, though." He handed the Santa figure to me. "Here. You try."

It was much lighter than I figured it would be. And up close, St. Nick's face didn't look as surly. Instead, he seemed . . . concerned. "What should I do?" I asked.

"Make a wish," Mr. Neighbor said.

I thought and thought. "Gosh, there's so many things I could wish for," I said. "I could ask for world peace or to have fresh-baked pie every day." I glanced at the wreath on the door. A small ceramic angel was sitting crooked amid the holly leaves. "Or to not be a silly Christmas angel."

"Not be a Christmas angel?" Mr. Neighbor repeated, looking confused.

I quickly told him about the tryouts and how we worked so hard and were truly the best, but that we didn't get to be the Wise Men because we were girls.

"That's a tough one, all right," he said, nodding. "Sometimes when folks are in the habit of seeing something one way, they just can't see it another way — no matter what. Some people can only think in terms of girl and boy, or young and old, or black and white."

Mr. Neighbor once told me that his great-great-great-grandfather (or maybe it was four greats, I can't recall) was a slave. When the slaves were emancipated after the Civil War, he moved his family to another part of Texas because, even though he was a free man, the people he'd been living with couldn't see him as anything but a slave. I wondered if that's what Mr. Neighbor was thinking about.

"Think my wish is too tough for St. Nick?" I asked.

He shrugged. "Wouldn't hurt to try."

I held the Santa figure gently in both hands and closed my eyes. "I wish that people could see things in lots of different ways and not just one or two. And, St. Nick? If you can't fix all the people, maybe just start with Mrs. Higginbotham."

Mr. Neighbor smiled. "If St. Nick can't help, I'm sure you smart girls will figure out a solution."

I remembered what Alex said about our being smart and how we could solve the dilemma of Mom's gift. It got me wondering about something. "Mr. Neighbor?" I said. "Is being smart the same as being wise?"

"Hmm." He glanced out at the yard in front of us and rubbed his whiskers again. After a while he shook his head. "I don't think so. You can be born smart. But you have to live and learn to become wise."

"But how do you learn from life?"

"By paying attention. By doing what you're doing right now — asking questions and listening." He grinned really big, and suddenly I could almost see him as a little boy.

It made sense, what Mr. Neighbor was saying. When you are on the United States Supreme Court, you help decide things that will affect the whole nation. To do this you have to know lots of facts about the cases you are reviewing, and about other laws and terms and rules. So you have to be smart. But you also have to ask questions of the people involved in the case, really listen to what they say, and then think long and hard before making your decision. That takes wisdom. You can have assistants help you look up the facts, but the questioning and listening and pondering all comes from you. So, I guess it's more important to be wise than smart if you're going to be a Supreme Court justice. But being both is best.

"St. Nick looks wise," I said, staring down at his long white beard and brooding eyes. "Maybe he'll be able to help after all." I handed it back to Mr. Neighbor.

"Just in case he can't, let's ask him for something easy. Like a piece of candy," Mr. Neighbor said. He held up the figurine so that it was looking straight at me. "Say it with me now. Say, 'I wish for a piece of candy.'"

"I wish for a piece of candy," I said along with him. I felt kind of silly. Sure, it seemed easier than wishing for Mrs. Higginbotham to realize she'd been unfair, but did he really expect a sugary treat to fall from the sky?

Mr. Neighbor placed a hand under the Santa's feet and started twisting gently. The next thing I knew, the legs had popped off the rest of the body! Mr. Neighbor tilted the lower half of the Santa toward me and I could see that it was a container. Sitting inside the bottom half of St. Nick were several small candy bars. I laughed in surprise.

"See? It came true," Mr. Neighbor said. "Have one."

"Thank you."

Soon Mrs. Neighbor came onto the porch. She carried a tray that held five cups of hot chocolate. Delaney and Dawn skipped along behind her.

I showed my sisters St. Nick. "It's priceless," I said. Then I made them wish for candy and Mr. Neighbor showed them the secret container inside the figure.

"Wow. Hot chocolate *and* candy," Delaney said.

Mrs. Neighbor handed out cups to each one of us and we all said, "Thank you, ma'am."

"Marshmallows all around?" she asked, holding up a plastic bag.

Dawn and Delaney both said, "Yes, please."

I said, "None for me. Thanks."

"She's weird," Dawn said. "She doesn't like marshmallows."

"Not even in hot chocolate, when they melt into a sweet foam," Delaney said. "But she is good at shooting them."

"Shooting them?" Mrs. Neighbor repeated, looking confused. She sat in one of the wicker rockers and patted the cushion on the chair next to her.

As I settled down beside her, I explained that one of my Christmas gifts from last year was a marshmallow shooter. It's kind of like a gun, but it doesn't hurt anyone.

"She's really good at it, too," Dawn said.

"Yeah! She can hit our drawing of Voldemort from really far away," Delaney said.

I smiled down at my feet, feeling shy but also proud that they were bragging about me.

Suddenly, Delaney was on her feet, pointing at the street. "Look, there's Lucas! Hey, Lucas! Hi!"

Sure enough, Lucas Westbrook was bicycling down the street. When he heard Delaney he looked both ways, crossed the road, and rode down the Neighbors' front sidewalk until he was right in front of us.

"What are you doing here? I thought you lived over there." He pointed across the street at our house.

"We do," Dawn said. "We're visiting."

"Mr. and Mrs. Neighbor, you know Lucas Westbrook, right? His house is the big white one on the corner," Delaney said.

Mr. Neighbor nodded. "I certainly do. I've waved at you many times as you've passed by with your parents in the car, or on your scooter, or on your bicycle."

"Yes, sir. But not this bicycle," Lucas said. "This is new, from my parents. I'm taking it out for a test drive. Isn't it cool?"

We all stepped to the edge of the porch to admire it. The bike was all shiny and silvery with a special compartment for Lucas's phone and a lockbox in the back for his valuable comic books and other things. It looked like the type of bicycle that would belong to a superhero. Or an undercover spy. Or a boy whose parents get him whatever he wants.

"My parents were so proud that I got in the pageant as one of the Wise Guys, they gave this to me after church on Sunday," he said.

Dawn, Delaney, and I exchanged sad faces.

Lucas must have noticed. "Don't worry," he said. "I'll share. You can come over and we'll take turns riding."

"Would you like some hot chocolate, Lucas?" Mrs. Neighbor asked.

He shook his head. "No, thanks. I need to get home soon. I'm supposed to get another present when my mom comes home. She's usually late, but I'm hoping she won't be today."

"At least have a candy," Delaney said. She turned to Mr. Neighbor. "Can we show Lucas the secret inside the Santa doll?"

"Why, sure," he said. He popped open the figurine and let Lucas choose a candy bar.

"Whoa. That's a cool Santa." Lucas smiled real big, and his braces gleamed like his new bike.

"It's priceless," Dawn said.

"It's the best Santa doll ever," Delaney said.

"It's magic," I said.

Everyone except Mr. Neighbor gave me a puzzled look, but I didn't mind. I liked having a secret wish.

If you got to be wise by living and learning, then maybe the St. Nick doll was incredibly wise. After all, he was very old and had seen a lot of life. Maybe that was where his magic came from. And just maybe, I would get my wish.

CHAPTER FOUR

Cabinet Session

Delaney

Our dad is a bachelor. That means he lives by himself and likes to eat off paper plates. His apartment is nice but small — only four rooms (two bedrooms, a bathroom, and a kitchen/dining/living area) — and it doesn't have a lot of things that Mom's house has. Like air freshener candles or covers for the tissue boxes or drinking glasses that match. The room we sleep in has a bunk bed, with a double mattress on the bottom and a twin mattress on top. My sisters and I take turns sleeping in the single bed, keeping careful track with records that we vote on for approval and store in a special file.

Dad's place does have things that Mom's house doesn't, though. Like a popcorn-making machine and old Star Wars movie posters, a robot vacuum cleaner we named Blanco, and a swimming pool that everyone in the building shares. Plus, he has the Vespa. It's like a cross between a motorcycle and a scooter, and Dad uses it for driving around town or short distances. We love it when he takes turns giving us rides. But when he has to drive a long way or pick up lots of people, he uses his Volkswagen bus.

That's what he was driving when he picked us up at the Neighbors' house. He was running late and apologized about fifty times. Then we picked up Quincy and his crate before heading to his apartment. We were excited because Quincy had never stayed at Dad's place before — he'd only visited on walks with us. We knew it would be a tight fit, but at least he'd be with us.

It took a while to find a place to put the crate, but finally Dad made an empty spot by moving his bins full of record albums. Records are the way people used to store music, only they're big and flat and the music is crackly and you aren't supposed to twirl or bounce near the record player or you might accidentally break the music. Also, the musicians on Dad's record covers are all spiky-haired, as if they'd just touched an electric fence. (Darby did that once and her hair puffed out like a peacock's tail.)

We don't mind that Dad's apartment is smaller or that his soap makes us smell like a pine forest. It's snug and fun — the kind of place where you aren't always nervous about where you put your feet.

What we were upset to see, though, was that he hadn't done any decorating for Christmas.

"Dad, where's your Christmas tree?" I asked.

He shrugged and gave us a weak grin. "Sorry. Haven't had time to put one up."

"But you said that when we were over two weeks ago — and two weeks before that," Dawn said. "Now there are just a few days left until Christmas."

"Sorry, girls," he said again. "Work has been crazy."

Dad is a medical device account manager. He goes to hospitals all over and sells special gadgets to surgeons. He also plays golf a lot, but it's all part of making a sale. Anyway, if people need to have surgery, they often schedule it for days close to holidays, so that they don't have to take lots of time off work. That means Dad is always busy around Christmastime, driving around to hospitals in Houston or San Antonio or Kerrville. This year he's been busier than usual.

"That reminds me," Dad said, snapping his fingers. "I need to get some things out of the van. I'll just be a sec. Make yourselves at home."

"Make ourselves at home?" Dawn said after he stepped through the door. She walked in a slow circle, studying the whole apartment. "He doesn't even have a stocking up. Or mistletoe. Or one lousy candy cane."

"It's like the Grinch was here," I said, also turning in a circle — only mine was a fast spin.

Even Quincy was wandering around whimpering. I couldn't tell if he didn't like it in the apartment, or if he was just picking up on our sulky moods. Maybe he could smell the soap.

"It's not Dad's fault that he's been busy," Darby said. "We shouldn't complain. So stop your bellyaching, Dawn, before you ruin our evening."

"It's not our fault, either," Dawn said. "I say we have a right to complain. We have to live here, too, and it's the holidays!"

Both of them had pink faces and narrow eyes. I knew what that meant. It was a sister standoff.

When you're a triplet, you can have lots of disagreements. When two of us are bickering, the third one steps in. So I'm used to times like these when Dawn is being cranky and stubborn, and Darby is being whiny and emotional.

As much as I don't like it, I also realize that it's probably good practice. The Speaker of the House of Representatives has to deal with standoffs all the time and make sure they don't stop work from getting done. Usually, the Speaker does this by coming up with ideas that might make everyone feel like they are winning — or that neither of them is winning. When it comes to Dawn versus Darby, I try different things. Sometimes, if I truly feel that one is right and the other is wrong, I take sides. Sometimes I broker a deal where one sister gets her way this time in exchange for the other sister getting her way the next time. Sometimes both of them can get a little bit of what they want, but not all. This is called a compromise, or a win-win. (It's also a lose-lose, but it's better to focus on the positive.)

But best of all is when I come up with an idea that isn't either of theirs but mine — one that they both like better than their own. This was one of those times.

"I have a proposal," I said, hopping on my toes. "What if we help Dad? We could get him some Christmas decorations when we're out shopping for presents tomorrow. That way we can find stuff we like and we don't have to bother him."

"Yes! Let's do that," Darby said.

Dawn tapped her chin. "I suppose that will work."

By the time Dad came back in, we all felt better. He was carrying a stack of boxes in his hands and steadying it with his chin. Dawn asked what was in them, and he smiled and said, "Knees and hips," so we knew they were work stuff and not presents for us.

When we were little, we used to think his job was kind of creepy. The kids at school would give us wide-eyed looks when we told them he sold metal pieces that became parts of people's legs and arms. But now we're proud that he helps people. We just wish he would let us have some of the hardware so we could try to build a robot.

"Who's ready for dinner?" he asked, setting the boxes in the coat closet.

"Me!" we said.

The three of us followed him into the kitchen, which was just a few steps away. We watched as he opened the refrigerator and kept saying "Hmmm" or "Uhhh."

"Sorry," he said as he squatted down to scan the lower shelves. "I'm afraid we don't have much. I was going to stop and buy burgers on the way to get you, but then I was running so late."

Neither one of our parents is what you'd call a gourmet cook. But they make a few things really well. Plus, Dad is great at finding deals at restaurants and Mom is good at getting things with coupons. But, leaning forward to peek inside, I couldn't remember if things had ever looked this pitiful. There was mustard and mayonnaise and half a quart of milk and six different kinds of barbecue sauce and three eggs in a carton, but no sandwich meat or cheese. We did find a bag of carrots, though.

I started looking through the drawers, hoping to find a pizza coupon or some granola bars or something. When we were at the house, we should have packed up food for us as well as Quincy.

"Wait! I've got it!" Dad called from inside a cabinet. "We'll have pancakes for dinner!" He held up a box of baking mix in triumph.

Dad put on an album of rock 'n' roll Christmas songs and we all helped make dinner. Soon we were sitting at the table, eating pancakes and carrot sticks off paper plates with jack-o'-lanterns on them. When we asked why he didn't use Christmas-looking plates,

Dad said he had a ton leftover from Halloween and that they work just as well. Then he apologized again and said not to worry, that he'd go shopping the next day.

"This is the perfect time to mention the presents we want," Dawn whispered when Dad got up to put on a new record.

"Because he keeps apologizing and feeling bad about Christmas?" I asked.

"Exactly," Dawn said.

"I don't know . . ." Darby said, her face all crimped and worried-looking. "Isn't that kind of taking advantage?"

"How bad do you want a zip line?" Dawn asked her.

Darby stared into the distance. Gradually, her worry lines disappeared. "Fine," she said. "But you go first."

In the background a lady started singing a bouncy version of "White Christmas." Soon Dad came back to the table.

"So, Dad," Dawn began. Her voice was soft and tinkly. "We know you're very busy, and you probably don't have a lot of time to mull over gifts for us. But that's all right, because we can give you pointers."

Dad raised his eyebrows. "You can?"

"Yep. Not a problem," Dawn said.

"We can just tell you what we want," I said, bouncing in my chair.

Dawn glared at me. "What Delaney means," she went on in her sweet fairy voice, "is why waste all that time wondering and searching? We can each give you suggestions and save you the trouble."

"I see." Dad was nodding and looking serious. He leaned forward on his elbows toward Dawn. "What sort of suggestions?"

Dawn tapped her chin. "Hmm. Let me think . . . Well, for example, if I had something like a — oh, what do you call those things? — a *megaphone*, I could help announce important information and summon the family when you need us to gather. It could be a very useful tool."

"Interesting," Dad said. "What about you, Darby?"

Darby cleared her throat and sat up straight. "A zip line would be a useful tool for learning coordination and balance. Plus, I'd be outside in the fresh air."

"Right." Dad nodded some more. He then looked at me. At that point I was practically dancing in my chair. "And you, Delaney? What do you need?"

"A mynah bird!" I said. "Mynahs can talk, so I can talk to it all the time and it can be my friend. I mean, I have friends and I have Dawn and Darby, but sometimes they get tired of talking, only a mynah bird probably won't."

Dawn gave me a bug-eyed stare.

"Um, also," I added, "I would learn responsibility taking care of the mynah bird."

"I can't give you girls any of those things. I'm sorry," Dad said.

"You sure are saying 'I'm sorry' a lot today," Dawn grumped. She crossed her arms over her chest and slouched down in her seat.

Dad looked stern for a second, then his face went sad. "Look, girls. The reasons your mother has for not getting you these gifts are the same reasons I have. Plus, I'm in an apartment, so there's even less room and more restrictions on noise and pets. Just look at poor Quincy."

Quincy was still pacing around, sniffing at everything he saw. He must have wandered into the bathroom at some point, because he had a tiny piece of toilet paper stuck to his nose.

"I love you girls," Dad said. "I love that you are curious and active and have excellent persuasive skills. I don't want that to change. But can you, maybe, think of some other gifts that you might like? It's true I could use the help."

He sounded so worn out and gloomy, I could hardly stand it. I looked over at Dawn and Darby and saw that their faces were crumpling.

"We're sorry!" Darby said. She leaped up from her chair and threw her arms around him.

"It's not your fault you're too tired for Christmas," I said, hugging him from the opposite side.

Dawn stood behind him and hugged him around his neck. "We shouldn't have tried to take advantage of your weakened state," she said.

Dad patted our arms. "Hey, I was eleven once. I know what it's like to want certain presents," he said. "Of course you would try to convert me to your cause. I'd expect nothing less."

"So what did you want when you were our age?" Dawn asked.

Dad gazed up at the ceiling and the right half of his mouth curled in a smile. "A pinball game and a drum set."

"Did you get them?"

He shook his head. "Neither one. For many of the same reasons I just gave you. But also . . . I wasn't as good a kid as you three are."

We continued hugging in a big group, and even Quincy came up and licked Dad's arm. Soon everyone was smiling and laughing and talking about what movie to watch that night.

I was glad we were going to help Dad with his decorations. And even though I was bummed that he said no to our gifts, at least we weren't all grumpy and gloomy anymore.

Starting the next day, everything would be more joyful and Christmas-y — I was sure of it. Even if all we did was eat off Christmas paper plates.

CHAPTER FIVE

Grassroots Effort

Dawn

The next morning Dad offered to go buy breakfast since we'd had pancakes the night before. Quincy was restless and whimpering, so we took him for a walk while Dad went for tacos.

It hardly ever snows where we live, and when it does it's usually only an inch or so. The last time it fell, we gathered all the snow in the front yard but could still only build a snowman the size of a squirrel. Still, our winters can get really chilly — to the point where you need to wear mittens, and your toes go numb inside your sneakers, and your nose turns red and runny. Quincy never seems to mind it, though.

We carefully crossed the main road so we could stroll around the neighborhood on the other side and admire the Christmas decorations. Everything was fine until Quincy peed on an elf statue at the front edge of someone's yard and a man came running out of the house. He was wearing a long housecoat, kind of like the Wise People's robes, but he didn't look wise. He just looked angry. The man hollered at us and we apologized on behalf of Quincy. I tried to explain that, in dog terms, Quincy was paying him a compliment, but the man didn't listen. Instead, he marched back inside and slammed his door so hard it made the PEACE ON EARTH sign fall off. We hurried away before he could yell at us for that, too.

Finally, Quincy did his business, and we made it back to Dad's place just as he was taking foil-wrapped tacos out of a white paper bag. I told him about the cranky man while Delaney fed Quincy and Darby refilled the water bowl.

"The holidays can be stressful, and people don't always act their best," Dad said.

"But it's supposed to be when people are merry," I said. "Like all the songs talk about. You know. Joy to the world. It's the most wonderful time of the year. You better not shout, you better not cry, you better not tattle on your sister."

"It's both. It's when people are happy because they are eating delicious food and opening gifts and spending time with loved ones. But it's also when people are anxious and frazzled from all the baking and shopping and decorating — and spending time with loved ones." Dad winked at me. "And remember, we also have stories and songs about grouchy people at Christmas. People like Ebenezer Scrooge and the Grinch."

"Yeah," I said. "And that dark-haired girl who yells at Snoopy and Charlie Brown."

"Her, too," Dad said. "People want things to be perfect, and they can never be."

I mulled over what he said as we ate our tacos. When Darby, Delaney, and I were little, Christmas was all about presents and cookies and pretty lights. There was a springy feeling inside us that grew stronger as Christmas came closer. Now that we're older, it's more complicated. We've already been disappointed with the whole pageant casting and Lily leaving and being told we wouldn't get the gifts we asked for. Was it tougher because this was just a lousy year, or because we were being more particular about what we expected? Maybe the older you get, the harder it is to feel that springy sensation.

Just as we were finishing our first round of bean and cheese tacos, Dad's cell phone rang, and we all perked up. I know the rest of them were thinking the same thing I was — that it was Lily and Mom calling from Boston. So we were really surprised when Dad said, "Good morning, Mr. Neighbor. How are you?" Then his face drooped and he went quiet. After a while he said, "I'm sorry to hear that."

Darby, Delaney, and I exchanged worried looks. Something was wrong with the Neighbors!

"Just a second." Dad lowered his phone and looked at us. "Mr. Neighbor is missing his antique Santa candy dispenser. You girls didn't see anything happen to it, did you?"

We shook our heads.

"It was on one of the porch tables when we left," Darby said. Delaney and I nodded in agreement.

Dad got back on the phone and told Mr. Neighbor what we said. He told him he hoped it turned up and said good-bye.

"Mr. Neighbor's old Santa doll is missing?" Darby asked once he'd hung up.

"Looks like it," Dad said. "They've searched everywhere but can't seem to find it. He was hoping maybe you had ideas."

"I wish we did," Darby said.

"Wait a sec," Delaney said. "If it isn't on their porch or in their house, and they didn't do anything with it, and we didn't do anything with it . . . then where is it?"

Dad shrugged. "I guess that means someone took it."

"But that's wrong!" I felt like that angry man from earlier — only I didn't have anyone to holler at. It made me want to open the front door and yell at the world.

"Did they call the police?" Delaney asked.

Dad nodded. "But I don't think the police can do anything. There was no property damage and no one was hurt. And really, it's a small item that's missing."

"But it's priceless!" Darby said. "It's been in Mr. Neighbor's family since before he was born! And he's already lived a long, long time!"

We talked Dad into letting us walk over to the Neighbors' house to check on them and see if we could help. He said he was happy we were being good friends to them, and he offered to drop us off since he needed to mail some orders and stock up on groceries. But he also made us promise not to get in the way and to be back at his place before lunchtime.

Mr. and Mrs. Neighbor looked surprised to see us twenty minutes later when we hopped out of Dad's van at the curb in front of their house.

"You didn't have to come all the way over here to check on us," Mr. Neighbor said. "We're fine."

"We wanted to offer support," Darby said.

"We can help you catch the culprit," Delaney said.

"And we can be witnesses when he goes to trial," I said.

"How nice of you," Mrs. Neighbor said. "Although I'm not sure how all that's going to happen."

The first thing we did was ask them to tell us everything they could remember. This is called getting the facts. Mr. Neighbor did the talking, since the St. Nick was his family heirloom, but we made sure Mrs. Neighbor was present to verify everything.

Mr. Neighbor said that after we left the day before, the two of them went inside to eat dinner. Delaney asked them what they ate and he said beef stew and corn bread. We all went "*mmm*" at this. Then they cleaned up the kitchen, watched some TV, locked up the house, and went to bed. It was early this morning when Mr. Neighbor realized St. Nick was missing. They looked all over their porch and house but couldn't find it. It wasn't in their car, either. The garden shed was locked and only Mr. Neighbor had the key, so it wasn't in there. And no one else had come over since we left — at least, not anyone they knew about.

"Well, that leaves just one explanation," Delaney said. "It looks like St. Nick was stolen."

"Ding-dang it!" I exclaimed. "This really has me steamed. I mean, who would do such a thing? It's so . . . so . . ."

"Mean," Darby said.

"Selfish," Delaney said.

"Un-neighborly!" I said.

I turned to Mr. Neighbor. "Did either of you see anyone suspicious that evening? You know, maybe on the street? Maybe wearing a dark cloak?"

They both shook their heads.

"Did you hear anything?" Darby asked.

Again, they shook their heads.

"Do either of you have any enemies?" Delaney asked.

"Delaney!" Darby scolded. "That's a personal question!"

"It's all right," Mrs. Neighbor said, laughing. "I understand this is part of the investigation."

"I can't say that everyone we meet is a big fan of us, but I don't think we have enemies," Mr. Neighbor said.

"Could . . . could, um . . ." Darby was talking in her shy voice. "Could St. Nick have disappeared on his own? You know . . . in a magical way?"

I thought that was the craziest notion I'd ever heard. I was just about to apologize on her behalf when Mr. Neighbor leaned toward Darby and said, "If St. Nick has those kinds of powers, he never showed them before. Not in a hundred years."

"I guess it's just one of those things," Mrs. Neighbor said. "We might never find out what happened, and that's all right. Life goes on."

I glanced around at each of them. They all had a sad *oh, well* expression on their faces.

"But we can't just give up! We have to do something," I said.

"Like what?" Delaney asked.

I wasn't exactly sure, so I thought for a moment about what professionals do in these situations. "Mr. and Mrs. Neighbor, would it be all right if we walked around your property, looking for clues?"

"That's very sweet of you. But I'm not sure what you'll find," Mrs. Neighbor said. "Wouldn't you rather help me make some gingerbread?"

"No!" I said — a little too loudly. Delaney had popped

up a couple of inches and I had to stop her before she accepted the invitation. "I mean, no, thank you. It's just that . . . We want to try to fix this. We need to. Don't you see? We can't let the Scrooges and Grinches win!"

Mr. Neighbor looked over at Mrs. Neighbor. "Well, I can't argue with that."

"Me neither," she said. "You girls go right ahead with your investigation. It is mighty nice of you to help."

"Yeah, well, it's probably our fault that the police weren't all that responsive," Darby said. "They've had a lot of false alarms from these parts."

Our other neighbor, Ms. Woolcott, is a bit of a freaker-outer. Whenever we get too loud with our assassination reenactments, or if Delaney gets spooked and lets out one of her intolerable screams, Ms. Woolcott calls the police. So it's true what Darby said. The cops are probably a little tired of being summoned to our block.

Mrs. Neighbor insisted that we have hot chocolate before roaming the grounds and, after a brief conference at the edge of the porch, we decided we would be more alert if we had extra nourishment and agreed to the offer. But we were quick about it. (Well . . . as quick as you can be drinking hot cocoa without burning your tongue.) A few minutes later we were outside, scouring the yard for anything out of the ordinary.

Mr. and Mrs. Neighbor have a pretty big piece of property. We walked hunched over — which isn't easy to do, by the way — scouring the front yard for any sort of clue. Like a footprint. Or tire tracks. Or a cigar butt — because I once saw a movie where a thief dropped the end of his cigar and they used it to track him down.

"Hey, look!" Delaney exclaimed. She ran over to me and Darby, cupping something in her hand. "I think I found a clue."

"It's a used Band-Aid," I remarked.

"We could test for DNA!" Delaney said, bouncing on her toes.

"Delaney, I think it's yours," Darby said. "It's one of the ones with Abe Lincoln on them."

"Oh." Delaney stopped bouncing. "It must have fallen off when we were playing in the sprinklers."

We went back to our search. After forty minutes of backbreaking work all we had found was the bandage, three hair ties, a piece of an ice-cream bar wrapper, and a couple of small rocks Darby thought were pretty.

"All of these things are probably ours from our sprinkler visits," I said. "Except for the rocks."

"Maybe the Santa-napper snuck onto the porch from the side or the back, instead of the front," Delaney said.

"Hmm . . ." I tapped my finger against my chin four times. "You have a good point. Let's go check around there."

We took a few steps toward the side yard when I realized it was just two of us. I turned around and saw Darby standing by the fence, staring off into the distance. I swear that girl can daydream like her life depended on it — which, of course, it never would.

I made a few loud *ahems* until Darby looked at me. "Why aren't you helping?" I asked.

"I was just thinking," she said. "Ms. Woolcott's house faces this direction. Maybe she saw something?"

CHAPTER SIX

Special Interest

Darby

While Mr. and Mrs. Neighbor do sweet and cozy Christmas decorating, Ms. Woolcott does big and flashy. It's as if she can't wait, too. Every year, the day after Thanksgiving, she sets out her yard art — big wire Christmas trees and reindeer that look like white skeletons in the daytime but have lights that flash and move at night.

The first week of December, we got a copy of her annual Christmas letter. Most of it was about her cat's diet, her foot surgery, and the excitement of a dear neighbor (Lily) who'd left her groom at the altar during a summertime wedding. "It's nice to be able to help neighbors in need," she wrote, which confused me. The only help I remember is the way she helped herself to most of the finger foods.

Mom said not to be too upset and that we should feel flattered that we figure so prominently in her life. She also said to be careful what we say around her.

"Why hello, girls! How are you on this lovely day?" Ms. Woolcott greeted us as she opened her door.

Ms. Woolcott was wearing a long green sweater that stuck out at the bottom, so that it looked like she was wearing a Christmas tree. All over the sweater were multicolored pom-pom ornaments, blinking lights, a shiny gold star at the top near the collar, and a long strand of tinsel that wrapped around her a couple of times. There was so much going on that it hurt my eyes — so I did what I usually do when I'm around her: I stared at her hair.

I'm always mesmerized by Ms. Woolcott's hairdo. It's truly a wonder. She somehow gets each strand to puff out a good two inches from her scalp and then adds enough hairspray to make a hardened shell, so it looks like she's wearing a motorcycle helmet made of hair.

"I hope we aren't bothering you," Dawn said.

"Nonsense. Come inside." She pushed her door open

wide and gestured with her arm. "Elvis, we have visitors," she called out.

Elvis is Ms. Woolcott's lazy old cat. He's gray with dark gray stripes and is super huge. All he does is lie around, look grumpy, and make a noise like "*myrrh*," which reminds me of one of the gifts to the baby Jesus.

"Would you like some homemade toffee?" Ms. Woolcott asked.

"Yes, please," we all said.

"Make yourselves comfortable and I'll be back with a snack." The colorful pom-poms bounced and swayed as she bustled off toward the kitchen, and the three of us headed into the living room.

It had been a while since we'd been in Ms. Woolcott's home. Usually, we talk to her at the fence that divides our property. Or she comes over because she's curious about a package we got or sees that we have company. I'd almost forgotten what her house looked like on the inside.

All of Ms. Woolcott's furniture has bright flowery material and curvy wooden legs, and she has lots and lots of paintings of flowers and hummingbirds on the wall. Everything is colorful and bold — especially now with her Christmas decorations up. She had not one, not two, but *three* Christmas trees. A big one by the front window covered with gold and silver balls, a medium-size one in the dining room covered with fake green and red apples, and a little one on a shelf over Elvis's bed covered in stuffed mice, hanging by their tails. Elvis didn't seem to notice or care about his tree. He lay on his poufy bed and watched us through the green slits of his eyes.

As we stepped farther into the room, I noticed even more color off to the side. On top of Ms. Woolcott's baby grand piano was a sparkly blanket of fake snow, and on top of that were dozens of Santa Claus figures.

"Hey, look!" I said in a loud whisper as I hurried over toward them. Dawn and Delaney came up on either side of me to see for themselves.

I'd never seen so many Santas in all my life. Some were regular Santas doing regular Santa things, like driving a sleigh or popping out of a chimney, but most were silly. There was one on a surfboard, one on a motorcycle, one ice-skating — even one behind a changing screen, wearing only boxer shorts covered with candy canes.

"What does it mean?" Delaney asked.

"It means Ms. Woolcott really likes Santas," Dawn said. "One might even say" — she glanced over her shoulder and lowered her voice — "that she has a weakness for them."

"What are you implying, Dawn?" I asked. I felt cold prickles. I didn't want to think bad thoughts about people who lived beside us.

"All I'm saying is, she has a collection of Santa figurines, and Mr. Neighbor is missing one of his." Dawn shrugged. "Is it coincidence? Or is it —"

Just then, I felt something slither against my legs. I let out a shriek and jumped back.

It was Elvis. He gave me an annoyed look and started licking his paw.

Ms. Woolcott came rushing into the room. One of her hands held a tin of toffee, the other was pressed against the gold star on her chest. "My goodness! Is everything all right?"

She looked really frightened. It was a good thing I screamed. If it had been Delaney, Ms. Woolcott probably would have passed out.

"I'm sorry," I said. "Elvis rubbed against my legs and startled me."

"He just wants to make friends. Don't you, Elvis?" she said. She set the tin of candy on her coffee table and walked over to pick up her cat. "Say hello, Elvis."

"*Myrrh,*" went Elvis.

"So how have things been, girls?" Ms. Woolcott asked as she plopped Elvis back onto his bed. "Tell me everything."

"Ms. Woolcott, I'm afraid we have bad news," Dawn said. "Were you aware that Mr. and Mrs. Neighbor were victims of a theft last night?"

Ms. Woolcott gasped loudly. "In our part of town? Why, no! That's horrendous! Ab-so-LUTE-ly shocking!"

I winced a little and leaned away from her. Ms. Woolcott doesn't talk so much as warble. She puts so much volume and melody into her words, you'd expect her to be holding a microphone and have a band playing behind her.

"I just can't believe it," she went on. "That's like a nightmare. It's . . . it's like a crime!"

"It *is* a crime," Dawn said. The way she peered at Ms. Woolcott reminded me of Elvis and the way he stared at people.

Ms. Woolcott kept shaking her head and clutching at her heart, as if too upset to speak. She gestured for us to sit on the couch in front of the coffee table and pushed the tin of toffee toward us.

"Such a shame," she said, plopping into the frilly armchair across from us. She gazed sadly in the direction of the Neighbors' house. "People need to feel safe in their homes. Don't you agree?"

We nodded.

"And what, may I ask, did the delinquents take?"

"A candy dispenser," Delaney said. "And all the candy inside it."

Ms. Woolcott frowned. "Beg your pardon? Is that all?"

"It's priceless," I said.

"But are you absolutely certain nothing else was stolen?" she asked. "No windows were broken? Their car is still there?"

We munched our toffee and told her we were absolutely certain. For some reason, Ms. Woolcott seemed kind of disappointed.

"Did you see anything?" Dawn asked, still making cat eyes at Ms. Woolcott. "What were you doing yesterday evening?"

"I didn't see a thing. I was out shopping. I needed to buy a baby and had to look all over for one."

Again, I felt cold prickles. "You . . . bought a baby?"

Ms. Woolcott noticed our stunned expressions and started laughing. Again, I shrank back from the noise.

Her laugh is kind of like Santa Claus's in that she goes "ho ho," but it starts out way up high, goes down a musical scale or two, and then climbs back up again. "For the king cake!" she explained once she could talk again. "It's my turn to bake a king cake for my women's group and I had to find a plastic baby — one that isn't a choking hazard — for the recipe."

"Oh." I was mighty relieved to hear it.

"What time did you return home?" Dawn said, continuing with her questioning.

"It was late," Ms. Woolcott said. "I'd say after nine."

"And you didn't see anything out of the ordinary?" I asked.

She shook her head. "Honestly, I don't know why you are going to all this trouble for just a trinket. It was probably just some spoiled, silly kids playing a prank."

"Maybe," Dawn said.

Ms. Woolcott then asked us all about Mom, Dad, and Lily and Alex and whether our family had gotten over the humiliation of the Almost Wedding last summer. We remembered what Mom said about being careful what we shared with her, so we didn't say much. We just told her everyone was fine and thanked her for her concern.

The topics were making me uncomfortable. So was the stiff-backed sofa. Beside me, Delaney was fidgeting and squirming as if she had fire ants in her pants.

"It's getting late, Dawn," I said. "We probably need to get back to Dad's place and walk Quincy, don't you think?"

Delaney was standing before I even finished my sentence. "Yeah, we should get going."

"I suppose you're right," Dawn said.

We thanked Ms. Woolcott for the toffee and the conversation and asked her to please let us know if she saw anything peculiar.

"Thank you so much for visiting. Please give my best to your family." She scooped up Elvis in her arms and waved his paw at us. "Say good-bye to the girls, Elvis," she said.

"*Myrrh,*" went Elvis.

As soon as we got outside we headed south toward town and Dad's apartment. Dawn walked lockstep with me, muttering under her breath, while Delaney, who's the fastest and had been sitting still for far too long, skipped in front.

"That Ms. Woolcott has got to be the nosiest woman in tarnation," Dawn grumbled.

"To be fair, you were asking her lots of questions, too," I pointed out.

"Gadzooks, Darby! Why do you always have to be so . . . so . . . *fair*. It's annoying," Dawn said. "But then again," she added with a sigh, "I guess that's why you'll be a great chief justice."

"Thanks," I said.

I walked in silence, letting myself feel good for a bit. Dawn doesn't give out compliments unless she really means them. So if you get one, you should take the time to enjoy it. Kind of like admiring a rainbow before it fades.

As we turned onto Dad's street, I said, "So . . . you don't really think Ms. Woolcott is guilty, do you?"

"She's never struck me as a low-life pilferer," she said. "But it does seem a strange coincidence that she collects Santas. Plus, she likes candy, too."

I had to admit it did look suspicious.

By now we were nearing Dad's apartment complex. "Dawn!" Delaney cried from way up ahead. "Toss me the key!"

Dawn took the Liberty Bell key ring out of her pocket and threw it toward Delaney, who ran forward and caught it.

"Thanks!" she shouted, and skipped toward Dad's building.

"Maybe we should forget about it for now," I suggested. "Let's look in on Quincy and then go get decorations for Dad's apartment. We could surprise him with —"

All of a sudden, we heard Delaney scream. And boy, that girl can scream. Dawn and I both froze for a second, staring at each other. Then I tore off running toward Dad's apartment while Dawn skedaddled back the way we came.

The door was open when I got there, and Delaney was standing just inside. I stopped right beside her, gazing in wonder all around.

Everywhere, there was snow. Well, not real snow, but the fuzzy white stuff that people use to stand in for snow when they decorate for Christmas in Texas. It was all over the floor and in tufts on the furniture.

Dawn, who must have overcome her fright and turned around, ran up beside me. "What happened?" she asked, out of breath. "Did Dad decorate?"

Delaney shook her head and pointed. All she could do was make little bleating sounds. *Delaney* — the gal who never stops talking. I knew something bad had happened. But all I could see was the back of the couch and that dad-blamed snow all over the place.

I cautiously stepped forward and rounded the couch. And that's when I saw it.

Quincy sat in front of the couch, looking guilty, a wisp of white sticking out of one side of his mouth. Beside him lay the ripped remnants of fabric.

It wasn't fake snow at all — it was the innards of Dad's couch. Quincy had torn it to shreds.

CHAPTER SEVEN

Great Compromise

Delaney

Dad hung up his phone, set it down on the table, and looked at it. "Well, that was the last one. I've called every dog boarding place, vet's office, and kennel in a fifty-mile radius, and none of them have openings."

Darby let out a wail. "We're sorry!" she said for about the sixty-seventh time before slumping onto the table-top and crying into her crossed arms. Darby always gets the hiccups when she's upset, so every now and then a loud "*hic!*" interrupted her bawling.

I was also sniffling and pacing around the dining room. Dawn was crying, too — although she kept trying to hide it and pretend she had a cold. She sat at the table next to Darby with an unfolded tissue over her face.

We felt so bad about what Quincy had done. Dad sure was surprised to come home and find the three of us weeping in the middle of his wrecked living room. We cleaned up the mess as best we could, but there was just no saving the sofa. It was a goner. The frame was kind of saggy to begin with, and the armrests had already been ripped. Now that our golden Lab had used it as a gigantic chew toy, it was just a bent skeleton of a couch with some shredded fabric still stapled to the frame in places.

Darby felt guilty that she hadn't latched the dog crate all the way. Dawn felt guilty because she'd been so worked up about the Santa-napper that she'd kept yelling at Darby to hurry up. And I felt guilty because I'd gotten Quincy all excited with some romping around right before we left. It was all our faults.

Dad kept saying "These things happen" and "It was just a cruddy old couch" to try to make us feel better, but he looked frazzled. His smile just wasn't as powerful and his whole face seemed saggy. We hadn't seen Dad this crumple-faced since the divorce. That was the worst part — and the main reason we were crying.

We're used to seeing strain and worry on Mom's face — that's just the way she is. She likes things neat and orderly and peaceful, and when they aren't that way she gets stressed out. In fact, sometimes we think she gets cross about things that aren't that big a deal. Dad, on the other hand, is more carefree. He doesn't mind messes as much and sometimes he forgets things. He shrugs things off pretty easily. So when Dad gets fretful, it means things are really bad. He'd already been under a lot of pressure because of work and the holidays, and now our sweet but senseless hound had to go tear up his home. We were the worst daughters in the world.

"I should have seen this coming," Dad said. "This is a different place with different smells, and it's a lot smaller than your mom's house. Quincy's whole routine has been changed up, so of course he would feel anxious being left alone here."

"But a kennel or boarding place would be new and stressful, too, right?" Dawn asked.

"Possibly," Dad said. "But they would have people there who could keep an eye on him all day. We can't do that."

"I'll do it," I said, hopping up and down and waving my arm in the air. "It'll be my job. And I'll do it for free!"

Dad gave me a small smile. "You can't, sweetheart. You girls told me you still had shopping to do. Plus, you have pageant rehearsal."

"Oh yeah. That," I grumbled. I stopped hopping and sat down at the table next to Darby.

"So what are we doing to do?" Dawn asked.

Dad let out a sigh. "I honestly don't know."

Darby let out another hiccup-y wail. I got back on my feet and started pacing again. I could hear Quincy whining from his crate. This was sure shaping up to be the most miserable Christmas in history.

Just then, Dad's phone started buzzing.

"It's your mother," Dad said, reading the display.

Darby wailed louder. Dawn ducked under the table. My pacing turned into a jog.

"All right, then. I'll say you three are busy." Dad took the phone into his bedroom and shut the door.

"We'll get grounded till next Christmas!" came Dawn's muffled voice.

Darby lifted her tearstained face. "She'll be so disa — *hic!* — disappointed in us!"

A terrible thought entered my mind. The kind of thought that creeps in the back, sneaks up behind you, and then grabs hold of you and won't let go.

"What if . . ." It was so awful, even I was finding it difficult to say it aloud. "What if Mom makes us get rid of Quincy?"

Darby stopped bawling and sat up straight. She stared at me in horror, her body shuddering every few seconds. Below her, Dawn peered out from beneath the green vinyl tablecloth. Her wide eyes and red-streaked face made her look like a clown fish darting out of an anemone.

A second later we were all running for Quincy's crate. We threw ourselves on top of it and started talking at once.

"She can't do that," Dawn was saying. "It wasn't his fault."

"It's — *hic!* — okay. We'll protect you," Darby was saying.

I just kept saying, "No. No no no no no no."

Quincy's head darted around, looking at each of us. His forehead was all crimped with worry and he let out a series of croaky whines.

I have no idea how long we stayed like that, but the next thing I knew Dad was gently lifting me off the crate. "It's okay," he said. Then he pulled Dawn and Darby off and told all of us to sit back down at the table.

"I spoke with your mom about what happened," he said.

Darby made a squawking sound, Dawn started to duck under the table again, and I was halfway to a standing position when he held up his hands and said, "Stop!" He waited for us to settle down before speaking again. "She was not happy to hear it, as you already predicted, but she's also come up with a solution."

"What?" I asked.

"She suggested that we all stay at the house. That way Quincy will be in more familiar surroundings and the four of us will have more places to sit."

None of us said anything for a moment. We were so stunned, we'd gone slack-jawed.

"Wow," Dawn said finally. "That's even better than one of my plans."

"So . . . we get to keep Quincy?" Darby asked.

Dad's eyebrows flew up. "Of course you do."

"What about your sofa?" I asked. "What about when you have to come back? You'll have no place to lounge and watch videos, or nap in the afternoons, or offer seats to company, or —"

Dad put his hand on my shoulder. "We'll worry about that later," he said. "None of us has time to deal with that now. Speaking of." He clapped his hands together. "Let's get all of our stuff and move right over.

That way we can settle in and get Quincy all set up before the pageant rehearsal. Deal?"

"Deal!" we all said.

Dawn and Darby scattered to pack up Quincy's stuff. I took off, too, but then did a circle and came running back. There was something I needed to say, and I needed to say it right then.

I came to a stop right in front of Dad. "Thank you."

"Uh . . . sure. For what?"

"For being our dad."

Dad grinned a tired grin. "That," he said, "is always my pleasure."

He still looked worn out, but his face had more lift and his eyes had more twinkle than before we found a solution. I really hoped this was a sign that things would get better.

Or at least that nothing else would go wrong.

CHAPTER EIGHT

Class Action Suits

Dawn

Making a fuss when you're mad could be called a big blunder. Making a fuss at church could probably be called a super-extreme mega blunder. And living in a small town means that if you make a big blunder, everyone will find out.

For example, you might think that if your parents aren't around, you could maybe get away with making a big blunder at the Christmas Eve Pageant rehearsal at church. But you would be mistaken. That is because of the smallness of our town. Lucas Westbrook lives down the road from us. The parents of Adam and Tommy Ybarra and Lucy Beasley hire my mom to do their bookkeeping. Wilson Cantu is cousins with Clare Silverman, who is Lily's best friend. Reverend Hoffmeyer has pie with our dad every couple of weeks. You get the idea.

But one of the good things about being a triplet is that your sisters can see when you are about to make a big blunder and know how to stop you. This is how I ended up locked in the crying room at the church.

It had been an abysmal, appalling, and catastrophic few days, so I was already in a sour mood. After we moved our stuff over to the house, we went to the church. Dad dropped us off because he needed to meet a client, so we were on our own. We walked the long sidewalk toward the glow of the main glass door when someone suddenly stepped out from behind the hedge and yelled, "Hey!" The three of us hollered. I staggered backward, Delaney took off like a shot, and Darby pushed the assailant back into the bush.

"Ouch!" the person said. That was when we recognized the voice. It was Lucas.

"Dagnabbit, Lucas! Why'd you have to go and scare us like that?" I asked.

"Why'd you have to shove me like that?" he whined.

"We had no idea it was you," Darby said. She stood over him and held out her hand to pull him back up. "It's dark and we couldn't see."

"I could see you! I just got these night vision goggles from my uncle for Christmas. That's what I was trying to show you," he said, pointing to his head. He was wearing a weird-looking helmet with big green goggles.

"Well, you could have picked a better way to do that," I grumped. "Besides, those goggles make you look creepy. Like a big fly with your wings plucked off."

We called out to Delaney, who had already made it to the other side of the church playground, and the four of us went inside.

I was still smarting from Lucas having scared us, and then he kept jabbering on and on about his latest gifts. That made me even crankier, since I knew we weren't getting what we wanted. All those bad feelings were piling on top of the others inside me — kind of like a lasagna, only not at all delicious.

Mr. and Mrs. Higginbotham were flanking the doors to the practice room. As we approached, Mrs. Higginbotham said, "Look, Bertram. It's the Brewster girls." Mr. Higginbotham nodded at us and went, "Uh-hmm."

Mr. Higginbotham doesn't talk much. In fact, when he speaks, he often doesn't use real words. He makes noises like *ohummmmm* and *heh* and *bah!*

"We're so happy that you three are going to be our sweet, lovable angels," Mrs. Higginbotham said.

This made me glower some more because I wanted to be a Wise Person, not a sweet angel, and I still thought the whole casting was a fiasco.

"That reminds me." Mrs. Higginbotham held up her hand. "Tell your mother to be sure and sprinkle a little cinnamon on the sugar cookies. It will give them more of a holiday flavor. Isn't that right, Bertram?"

Mr. Higginbotham made an "*mmmm*" noise, maybe to say that he agreed. Or maybe to say that he really liked cinnamon on his cookies. I wasn't sure.

I was tempted to tell Mrs. Higginbotham to mind her own beeswax, so instead I pursed my lips and sucked in my cheeks to keep the rude words in my head.

The second we entered the room, Adam came up and said, "What noise does a camel make?"

Darby, Delaney, and I exchanged puzzled looks. "What do you mean?" I asked.

"You know. Like, a horse goes . . ." Adam threw back his head and made a long whinnying sound. "And a donkey goes . . ." He made a loud hee-haw sound. "But how does a camel go?"

"I have no idea," I said.

"Me neither," Delaney and Darby said at the same time.

Adam seemed really disappointed. "I thought you guys were smart."

I made a growly noise — a quiet one, but loud enough for Darby to hear. Hearing Adam say that was like another layer on my bad-feelings lasagna.

"You aren't going to lose your cool, are you, Dawn?" Darby whispered.

"Of course not," I said, which was kind of a lie, since by that point I wasn't positive I could control my temper. I was trying really hard, but it wasn't my fault so many people around me were acting like nitwits.

As soon as everyone had arrived, Mrs. Higginbotham showed us a rack with a bunch of different-colored robes hanging on it. One by one she handed each of us a robe and told us to put it on over our clothes.

"You three have the most beautiful ones!" she said to me, Darby, and Delaney. Lying across her arms were three robes made out of some sort of white silky stuff with sparkles on it.

Mr. Higginbotham had a box of other props. He gave fake beards to Lucas, Adam, and Tommy, and animal ears to the younger kids. We each got a pair of white wings with big stretchy bands that went over our robes and a gold headband attached to a halo.

"I feel ridiculous," I muttered, staring at my reflection in a nearby window.

Delaney twisted from side to side. "The wings stop the robes from twirling right," she said, sounding disappointed.

Darby was doing an up-and-down motion. "I wonder what would happen if I were to jump out of a tree with these wings on," she said.

"Don't even think about it. There's no way these fake things will allow you to fly," I said.

Darby looked shamefaced. "I know. I just thought they might work as a parachute and slow down my fall."

It took a few minutes for everyone to get ready. Lucas wanted to wear his night goggle helmet, but Mrs. Higginbotham said no. And one of the little kids got his head stuck in a robe that was way too small for him.

Finally, we got to the dumb rehearsal. Mrs. Higginbotham had us go into the sanctuary so we could run through the play on the stage.

I just wanted to get it all over with, but Mrs. Higginbotham kept doing things badly. It was bad enough that we had the wrong parts, but her directing was half-baked, too. Instead of focusing on how people acted, she was all hung up on how people looked.

For example, she'd say, "Lucy, I've changed my mind. I think the blue robe is more becoming on you. And Lucas, you would look better in the green." Then they'd switch costumes and we'd run the play again.

After a while, everyone's hair was standing on end from having to pull robes over their heads. Our braids would have stuck out like Pippi Longstocking's, except that we were the only ones who never had to switch costumes. We just had to stand there and sway and sway and sway — or, rather, I was swaying, Delaney was twirling, and Darby was just standing there because all that pitching to and fro made her feel seasick.

Meanwhile, Wilson and Lucy kept making faces and wouldn't stand next to each other because they were in a fight. And the kids playing animals reminded me of mini versions of Delaney, the way they kept bouncing about and spinning to watch their robes flare out. But what really got me steamed were Lucas, Adam, and Tommy. Every time they had to trudge toward the manger to present their gifts, they did it in a silly way. They danced, walked hunched over like really old people, swaggered like cowboys, hopped like frogs — everything except look noble and reverent. Plus, they wouldn't do their lines right on purpose. Instead of gold, frankincense, and myrrh, they'd announce gifts like a video game console, a skateboard, and a trip to Disneyland. It was extremely unprofessional — and annoying.

The rage lasagna inside me was getting bigger and hotter, and I had half a mind to go kick them all in the shins. But I didn't. Mainly because there was a bright side to their shenanigans: I felt sure that sooner or later Mrs. Higginbotham would get fed up with their behavior, maybe to the point where she'd give the roles to more deserving folk.

Finally, Mrs. Higginbotham seemed satisfied with the costumes.

"All right. Now we will start hemming your outfits," she said. "That's enough rehearsal."

I was so surprised, I thought my jaw would come unhinged. "What? That's it? No more practicing?" I asked.

"Yes, I promise. You can all relax now," Mrs. Higginbotham said, smiling at me as if she were certain I'd be happy with the news. "I'll go fetch my sewing kit and call you up one by one."

"But . . . but . . ." All I could do was stammer and (according to Darby and Delaney) turn the same color as holly berries.

"What's up with Dawn?" I heard Delaney mutter to Darby. "She looks like she's about to spit fire."

"Stay cool, Dawn," Darby said. "Think about Dad."

I thought about Dad and the whole awful episode with Quincy earlier that day. I could suddenly understand why Quincy would feel so frustrated at having been left behind and ignored that he would mangle an enormous piece of furniture.

"Darby Brewster," Mrs. Higginbotham called out. She stood at the front of the room and held up a needle and thread. "You will be first. Come up here and let me hem your robe."

Darby hesitated. She studied me closely, as if counting every freckle. Then she said to Delaney, "Keep an eye on her," and headed toward Mrs. Higginbotham.

The thing about having Delaney in charge of something is that she won't be able to do it for long — especially if it involves being still. So while I slouched in a pew with my arms crossed, she kept a watch over me — for about three minutes. Then she moved down the pew by walking her arms down the pew backs, letting her feet swing off the floor. Before long, she was three pews over, doing something else.

"Hello, Mrs. Higginbotham," someone called out from the back of the room. I knew that voice well. It was Reverend Hoffmeyer.

I watched as he strode halfway down the main aisle, greeting everyone he saw. Just the sight of him made me feel a little better. Reverend Hoffmeyer has been our minister our entire lives, and we like him a lot. He's always happy to listen and never talks to us in that phony adult way where they are laughing on the inside and just pretending to take you seriously.

A plan started to form in my mind.

"Hellooo, Reverend," Mrs. Higginbotham called out. "To what do we owe this honor?"

The reverend lifted his hand and shook his head. "Nothing formal. I was just working late and thought I'd peek in and have a look. I don't want to be a distraction."

"You are quite welcome," Mrs. Higginbotham said.

As soon as she focused back on her sewing kit, I sped over and stood right in front of the reverend. "Hello, Reverend Hoffmeyer," I said.

"Hello, Dawn. Are you looking forward to Christmas?" He smiled big, revealing that tiny gap between his front teeth. I always liked that little space. It's like his teeth are pulling apart ever so slightly to allow his enlightened words to come out more easily.

I shook my head. "So far the holiday has been a huge disappointment, but that's not what I'm here to discuss," I said.

I'm ashamed to say I was kind of hasty while chatting with him. I was trying not to let the mad feelings about the pageant take me over. But even though I wasn't hollering, I was still antsy and impatient and bent on getting my way.

"I see," he said. "What can I help you with?"

"I was wondering about something, Reverend," I said. "Angels aren't all female — right?"

"Well, that's true. They're . . . different sorts of beings. Why —"

"And women are just as wise as men, right?"

"Well, yes. Of course they are. Why do you —"

"Thank you, Reverend Hoffmeyer," I said, turning to leave. "This was a very helpful talk. I feel better now."

As I hurried off, I could hear him say, "Oh, um . . . That's good to hear. Anytime. Carry on, children."

I trotted right over to Mrs. Higginbotham, who was now sticking pins in the bottom of Adam's robe while Adam played games on his phone.

"Mrs. Higginbotham, I need to tell you something important," I said.

"Just a second, dear," she said. She stuck in another pin, gave the end of Adam's robe a gentle tug, and stood up straight. "That was the last one, Adam. Take it off carefully." As she helped him duck out of his robe she turned to look at me. "Yes, sweetie? What is it?"

I looked all around me, leaned forward, and whispered. "Only a few seconds ago, Reverend Hoffmeyer was saying that males are just as good at playing angels as females. I think he was making a big hint about the pageant casting."

"What? I don't understand. Reverend Hoffmeyer wants to play an angel in the pageant?"

I couldn't believe my ears. "No! What he meant was —" I was just about to set her straight when Darby came up on my left and grabbed my arm. In a flash, Delaney came up on my right.

"Excuse us for a second, please, Mrs. Higginbotham," Darby said. "We need to talk to our sister. It's urgent."

"No! Wait! I need to tell her!" I kept protesting as they frog-marched me down the aisle and steered me through a nearby door, closing it behind them. Inside were a couple of rocking chairs facing a thick window that looked onto the sanctuary. As my eyes adjusted to the light from the stage, I could see blocks and plush toys strewn on the carpet.

We were in the room that allowed parents with crying babies to see the church service.

"You've got to calm yourself down," Darby said.

"Yeah. Dad is under enough pressure and you're about to go all ... all ... *Dawn* again!" Delaney said. "If he hears that you've been causing a ruckus he might explode from all the hassles he's having to deal with."

"I'm fine!" I said — maybe a little too loudly.

"No, you're not," Darby said. "And I can't believe you were about to use Reverend Hoffmeyer in one of your outrageous schemes!"

Delaney gasped. "You were?"

"No! Well ... sort of." I took a big breath and started marching all around the room. "I just can't stand it! I quit this sham of a show!" I took off my halo and flung it into a corner. "Those boys are doing it all wrong, and that crazy lady is letting them! We deserve those parts! Not them!" Next, I wriggled out of the wings (which wasn't easy) and tossed them behind me. Last, I pulled the sparkly robe off, wadded it up, and tried to toss it — but because it was so light it didn't go that far, which was really unsatisfying.

Delaney scurried about, picking up the pieces of my discarded costume, while Darby just stood and watched me with wide, worried eyes. As I stopped to take a breath, I noticed that Darby's hair was down. It stood out from her scalp in zigzaggy kinks from having been in a braid all day.

"Why is your hair like that?" I asked.

Darby looked down at the floor. "Mrs. Higginbotham doesn't want us to wear braids at the pageant. She says they aren't elegant."

"I heard her say that, too," Delaney said. "She's going to bring her curling iron and try to give us ringlets."

The noise I made next is a point of debate. Darby says it sounded like a riled-up mountain lion. Delaney says it sounded like a bugle charge into battle — only off-key and way scarier. Me? I don't even remember making a noise. All I recall is a hot rage spreading through me.

The bad-feelings lasagna had gone kablooie.

"That's it!" I hollered. "Of all the lamebrained, crazy-pants, dunderheaded notions! I'm going to march right out there and —"

"No!" Darby and Delaney cried out. As I made a move for the door they stood in front of it, blocking my path.

"We don't like it, either, but you're only going to make it worse!" Delaney said.

"You just need to stay in here and calm down!" Darby said.

I had to do something with my anger, but my mind was still intact enough to not mess with my sisters. Instead, I marched around the room, kicking stuffed animals and griping about the lack of fair representation within the church youth and how there ought to be a rule or a law or a commandment. As I came to the end of my circle I turned toward the door and saw that Darby and Delaney were now on the other side, watching me through the rectangular window.

"Let me out!" I said, trying to turn the handle.

They shook their heads.

"We're intervening for your own good!" Darby said.

"Yours and ours and Dad's and the whole family's!" Delaney said.

And that's how I ended up locked in the crying room.

CHAPTER NINE

Isolationism

Darby

It's a frightening sight watching Dawn lose her temper. She can be hotheaded, and we're used to that. But when she gets in an all-out dither, it's like having an up-close view of a lightning storm.

Delaney and I knew the minute we arrived at church that we had to keep an eye on her. The three of us were still tormented by the events of the day — the Santa-napping and Quincy's bad behavior — but Dawn didn't seem like she was calming down. And after Lucas scared us, Dawn had that exact look in her eye that a rooster gets right before he tries to peck you in the knee-caps. We knew that if anything else went wrong, she would blow.

Dawn doesn't mean to fly off the handle — really. Afterward, she always feels bad and apologizes for most of it. But with all the other things going wrong for Dad, we didn't need to have another incident at church.

I say *another* because a couple of years ago I tried to jump a bicycle over a watermelon at one of our spring picnics and ended up in the hospital. It was a dare. Apparently, head wounds bleed an awful lot, even if you don't actually crack your skull. And some people automatically faint at the sight of blood. So now the newsletters specify that melons should be brought in slices to any church gatherings.

Even though we knew that later on Dawn would forgive us, and maybe even thank us, she sure was riled up when we made her stay in the crying room. It's a good thing the walls are soundproof. She was able to rant and rail and call us names like "ferret-faced Benedict Arnolds" and we were the only ones who could hear her muffled voice. We figured all we had to do was wait for her to run out of steam.

And then Mrs. Higginbotham called out, "Dawn Brewster? Get ready, Dawn. As soon as I finish with Wilson, it's your turn to get hemmed!"

Delaney and I traded worried faces.

"What do we do?" I whispered. "No way can we let Dawn out of there and anywhere near Mrs. Higginbotham. Especially with all those sharp needles. She's probably never putting that robe on again." I pointed at her costume pieces, which were lying in a heap beside us.

"How about I go and pretend to be Dawn?" Delaney suggested.

I noticed the way she was squirming. "Actually . . ." I said. "Maybe I should go. And I'll also pretend to be you when it's your turn. You stay here and guard the door."

We quickly shook hands on it and she slipped out of her costume. She gave me her shoes to help with the deception. When you're a triplet, people tend to focus on the things that are different about you — hairstyle, an item of clothing, or even a stray eyebrow hair — in order to tell you apart. So we learned long ago to incorporate these variations if we ever wanted to transform into one of our sisters.

Luckily, a couple of the younger kids had started messing with the organ, and Mrs. Higginbotham was telling them about the thousands and thousands of dollars it cost. That bought me time to put on Dawn's costume and quickly re-braid my hair. I hunched over and ran the length of the back pew so that no one would see me. When I was sure the coast was clear, I snuck around to the backstage area. I stowed Delaney's costume and shoes and tried to put a Dawn-like expression on my face (brows lowered, eyes slightly narrowed, head tilted to the right). Then, when Mrs. Higginbotham called for her again, I stepped out from backstage.

"Here I am, Mrs. Higginbotham," I said.

"Oh, there you are, Dawn," she said. "Come over here and stand just so."

I took my spot next to the steps, where she was sitting, and tried to act like I hadn't been through the whole rigmarole before. I stood "just so" like she told me and kept an eye on the dim corner where Delaney was guarding the door to the crying room. It was tougher standing still the second time, and I was just starting to feel wiggly when I heard a buzzing sound.

"Oh dear. Excuse me one second, please." Mrs. Higginbotham stood and pressed a cell phone to her ear. "Hello? . . . Oh, hello, Theresa. With all due respect, I am rather busy. I'm at church, doing . . . What's that? You don't say! You don't say!"

That's a phrase Mrs. Higginbotham often uses that baffles us. Obviously, Theresa *was* saying these things, and I couldn't understand why Mrs. Higginbotham kept insisting that she wasn't.

"I agree," Mrs. Higginbotham went on. "Christmas has become an excuse for people to put out the ugliest decorations imaginable. Far be it from me to complain, but something should be done, and our city officials are useless in this regard."

I realized I was eavesdropping. Mom had a serious talk with the three of us about eavesdropping and spying after we meddled with Lily's wedding plans. But how do you not eavesdrop if someone has a conversation right in front of you — and you can't leave because you have sharp pins sticking out of your clothes and you were told to stand "just so"?

"Anything in poor taste should be snatched right up, I say," Mrs. Higginbotham went on. "We simply can't have ugly decorations and still have a beautiful town."

A prickly sensation swept over me, as if Mrs. Higginbotham were jabbing me with hundreds of pins instead of sitting on the step beside me, yakking on her cell phone.

My brain was cranking out a series of awful thoughts: Mrs. Higginbotham thinks she's in charge of how everything looks — and not just with the pageant . . . Mr. Neighbor was missing his Santa figurine . . . Mr. Neighbor's Santa wasn't ugly, but he was old and had kind of a severe look on his face and he wasn't dressed up in a fancy red suit like other Santas . . . Having the right costume was obviously super important to Mrs. Higginbotham . . . Mrs. Higginbotham was talking as if she wanted people to steal Christmas decorations she thought were ugly . . .

I suddenly felt really uncomfortable, and it wasn't just because I was standing like a statue. It was as if each of those notions in my head were a link in a chain, and I kept following the chain even though I knew it would lead to a big, dreadful beast of a thought. Eventually, I came to it:

Could Mrs. Higginbotham have had anything to do with Mr. Neighbor's missing Santa?

"I have to go, Theresa. I'll call you later," Mrs. Higginbotham said. "Remember, at the end of the day, any steps we take will benefit the entire town, not just us."

Mrs. Higginbotham turned off her phone and slipped it back into the pocket of her skirt. She shook her head and made a *tsk-tsk* sound with her tongue. "Some people just don't have good taste. Oh! That reminds me." She stood and looked right at me. "I need you girls to please wear your hair down for the pageant."

She went on and on about looking elegant and how we were putting on a pageant with class — blah, blah. Again, I tried to pretend I was hearing it all for the first time. I undid my braids and listened to her go on about curling irons being miracle workers. If I had really wanted to act like Dawn, I would have argued with her about our hairstyles being important, but I was way too shy and way too eager to be done.

Also, I just didn't have the stomach for it. Literally. My insides were still wriggling around after that phone call I accidentally overheard. All I wanted to do was scurry away and consider the whole mess — like a Supreme Court justice retiring to her chambers.

"There you go," Mrs. Higginbotham said, straightening up. "Take off your robe very carefully and go tell Delaney that it's her turn."

"Um . . . okay, but . . . um . . . it might take a while," I said, ducking out of the robe as Mrs. Higginbotham held on to the top of it. "Because . . . um . . . because . . . Delaney had to go to the bathroom." I was so glad Mrs.

Higginbotham couldn't see my face, because I'm awful at lying. I don't just mean of the three of us — I'm probably the lousiest liar of any person ever born.

"Very well, then. I'll do the donkey's tail next. Please go find Delaney and tell her to hurry."

I nodded, trotted down the steps, and then, when she wasn't looking, I slipped back into the shadows at the side of the stage. All I had to do was find where I stashed Delaney's robe and go through the hemming process again. As much as I didn't want to, I also knew it was probably for the best. Delaney had her hands full with Dawn — which, luckily, seemed to be going all right, considering I hadn't heard a peep since I'd left them. But also, there was no way Delaney would be able to stand still while Mrs. Higginbotham hemmed and chattered. I was probably sparing everyone from a bloody mishap. And maybe a fainting spell or two.

I found where I'd hidden Delaney's angel robe and quickly wriggled into it. I had just started to braid up my hair again when I heard someone make a throat-clearing sound. As my eyes got used to the dim light, I could see a figure in the cubicle where the sound equipment is kept.

It was Mr. Higginbotham. He was sitting on a stool

behind the curtain, holding an electronic tablet in both of his hands. Some sort of basketball game was on the screen.

He saw me notice the screen and grinned. Then he held a finger in front of his mouth and went, *"Shhhh."*

I smiled back and nodded. As I did, a few clumps of hair, all catawampus from having been braided all day, danced in front of the left side of my face. And I realized that I only had one side braided.

I wasn't sure if he knew about our ruse — or if he was even aware that one was afoot. But just in case, I grabbed a clump of crooked hair and waved it at him. *"Shhhh!"* I went.

He nodded back.

CHAPTER TEN

Market Research

Delaney

The next day, as we walked into town to do our Christmas shopping, we reviewed the events from the night before. Dawn was feeling a little shamefaced about her outburst at church. She was mostly calmed down but still sounded testy about the pageant and the terrible job that Lucas, Adam, and Tommy had done. So Darby and I tried to focus on the missing Santa and the theory Darby had come up with after accidentally listening in on Mrs. Higginbotham's phone conversation.

"It's intriguing, all right. And that lady's already on my bad side, so I'm tempted to make her a suspect anyway," Dawn was saying as we stopped to wait for a WALK sign. "But it's not like the Neighbors' house is in view of Mrs. Higginbotham's house — in fact, I'm not even sure where she lives. Plus, that Santa doll wasn't huge. I don't think anyone could see it from the road."

"But you should have heard her," Darby said. "She got all worked up about how people don't know how to do decorations right. Maybe she stopped by their house, saw it, and just lost her cool and did something stupid?"

"Well, I do know about things like that," Dawn said, sounding sheepish. She made her eyes big and round in a *so sorry* look.

I tilted my head and grinned to let her know I wasn't sore at her — although I was a little sore. That is, my shoulders hurt from having to push hard against the door of the crying room the couple of times she tried to force her way out. But I wasn't going to tell her that.

The part of Dawn that makes her throw tantrums is the same part that makes her fight hard for justice and never give up — which is a good quality to have if you want to lead a nation.

It's sort of like . . . fire. It can burn you and tear down buildings and stuff, but it can also keep you warm and give off light when it's dark. It's not all good or all bad, it just depends on how it's used. So I guess people need to learn how to use the fires inside them.

When I told my sisters about this thought, Dawn said it sounded like hooey, but that she kind of understood what I meant. She said she definitely has fires inside her — loud, angry ones. Then she said something about exploding lasagna.

Darby said it sounded very smart. Then she shook her head and said, "No. Not just smart — wise."

That made me bounce extra high.

The day was a little warmer than before and there was more wind. I love blustery days. It's like the air is running around in a big hurry. It makes me feel extra alert. A few big brown leaves scampered across the street with us as we headed to Goldie's Department Store, and I skipped along with them.

Goldie's is one of my favorite spots in Johnson City. It's got wood plank walls and wood floors and wooden shelves and tables covered with just about everything you can think of. And they always make it look so pretty and colorful. The front part usually smells like flowers, because they have a whole section with buckets full of different-colored blooms. But in December that area smells like Dad's soap because of all the wreaths and other things made out of evergreen branches.

I took a deep breath as we walked inside and, sure enough, the air smelled like pine and peppermint.

"Delaney, quit bouncing," Dawn scolded. "You're going to knock stuff over."

That's the only bad thing about Goldie's. I like it so much, my arms and feet do dances — which sometimes makes me knock into things. When we were shopping for Lily's birthday present in September, I accidently bumped a display of basketballs and caused an avalanche.

"Stick to the wide aisles," Darby said to me.

As we made our way through the store, I noticed that the shelves and tables weren't brimming with as much stuff as they usually had — a reminder that there wasn't much time left before Christmas and that most people had finished buying their gifts.

Luckily, we were almost done with our shopping. The three of us had bought Dad a pillow shaped like an electric guitar, a bracelet for Lily, and a paperback of presidential trivia for Alex. Darby and I got Dawn a kit where you can build a scale model of the White House. And Dawn and I got Darby a thousand-piece puzzle of the Declaration of Independence. I'm not sure what Dawn and Darby got me, but I'm sure I'll like it. They know me pretty well.

As per usual, the one present we had left to buy was the one for our mom. We hadn't had any luck so far, but today we were only focused on that gift, so we felt more hopeful.

First, we went to the ladies' section in Goldie's and looked at anything that was in our price range, which mainly ended up being scarves and gloves and hair clips. Only we've never actually seen her wear scarves and she already has two pairs of gloves. Plus, Mom keeps her hair really short.

Next, we went to the perfume section. Well . . . Dawn and Darby went to the perfume table and told me to stay by the scarves and other soft things — far away from the breakable stuff. I could see them sniff a few bottles. Then a lady came over and sprayed one for them. Dawn made a big face and Darby started sneezing, which turned into the hiccups.

"Forget that," Dawn said in a wheezy voice as they came back for me.

"Everything — *hic!* — reminded me of Ms. Woolcott's house," Darby said.

I was starting to feel discouraged, and then Dawn called an emergency meeting over by the wrapping paper. "Let's do one last brainstorming session before we give up on this place," she said. "Think. What can we get Mom that would make her happy or make her life easier?"

We pondered and pondered until it felt like I was squeezing my brain from all sides, but for a long time no one said anything. Finally, Darby suggested we get her a lasso so that she could catch Quincy when he was in one of his stubborn moods and refused to come back, and Dawn suggested we get her one of those iron triangles that people beat on to call people home for dinner. That way, Mom could use it to call us when we were out romping in the Neighbors' sprinklers. But when we stopped the sales lady and asked her if they had either of those things, she said we needed to try someplace else.

Then, suddenly, I got an idea. "Excuse me, ma'am," I said before the sales lady could walk away, "but do you have those kinds of bath salts that make your whole house go quiet and the birds come sing at your window?"

The lady looked confused. "You mean like that commercial?" she asked.

"Yes!" I said, bouncing on my toes.

"No, we don't carry those," she said with a *so sorry* smile. "But also, those salts don't really do that."

I stopped bouncing.

"It was worth a try," Darby said, patting me on the arm.

We did end up making one purchase before we left. We got a fake Christmas tree that was on sale for Dad. Even though we'd already bought him a present, we figured he could use it. The tree is only a couple of feet high, just right for his apartment, and looks like it was made out of shiny tinfoil.

"This way he won't have to buy a new one each year," Darby said.

"And it's cool and sci-fi looking!" I said, hugging the bag with the boxed-up tree in it to my chest and spinning around.

"And it was on sale!" Dawn said.

Finding a Christmas decoration for Dad made us feel a little better about not finding anything for Mom. But as we stepped out onto the street, we stood there for a moment, looking at each other, and our smiles went away. It wasn't as breezy outside anymore, and I wondered if the day had lost its pep, like we had.

"What now?" Darby asked.

"I have no idea," Dawn said. "I hate it when I have no ideas."

"Maybe we can find a place that sells lassos or triangle dinner bells?" I suggested.

Dawn tapped her finger against her chin, the way she always does when she's thinking hard. "I know," she said. "Let's split up and each go a different direction. That way we can cover more ground in less time. Since we came from the north and will head back that way, I figure there's no need to bother with that direction. Darby, you go east. Delaney, south. I'll head west. After half an hour, even if you haven't found anything, head to the courthouse and we'll meet by the cannon."

Darby and I agreed, and we each took off in our separate directions.

I crossed the street and headed south, passing a gas station, a flower shop, and an empty building. As I neared the corner, I could see Buck's Bazaar, a fenced-in yard that sells lamps, swings, and art made out of metal. It's super cool. On the roof is a gigantic sculpture of a horned toad, which I really wanted — only I guess they weren't selling it since it was way up on the roof. We drive past the horned toad all the time and it always makes me smile. I really wanted to get Mom something that would make her smile.

I went into the shop and had fun looking at the other metal sculptures — and was glad I didn't have to worry about bumping them accidentally. But even though I had fun looking, I didn't have enough money to buy anything. When I left, I stood on the street and realized I'd gone as far as I could go. The only other things south were the visitor's center and the Lyndon B. Johnson National Historical Park. Both were cool places but probably not where I'd find a Christmas present.

As I trudged back toward the center of town to meet my sisters, I noticed a store on the other side of the street. I'd gone right past it earlier. It was third in a row of wood-front shops, the skinniest of them all. Above the doorway, a painted sign read KITSCH KINGDOM. I peered inside and saw lots of dolls, doll furniture, some antique chairs, and some Styrofoam heads with wigs on them. All those dolls and wig heads staring back at me made me go "*Eeep!*" and I almost turned around and left speedy quick. But then, sitting on a table near the entrance, I saw what looked like a banana wrapped in plastic. A label said, SCREAMING BANANA!

Screaming Banana? This I had to see.

I carefully stepped inside and picked it up. All at once it made a noise like *"Aaaaaaugh!"* which made me yelp — then laugh. I turned the banana a different direction and it went *"Eeeeeeeuah!"* Then I turned it again and it said, "Whatsamatta? You don't find me a-peeling?"

A man behind the counter said, "Are you going to buy that?" His voice was kind of weary-sounding.

"How much is it?" I asked.

"Eight dollars."

"Sold!"

He seemed a lot more cheerful once I bought it. I even told him not to bother with a bag and put it in with the tinsel tree. As I skipped to the meeting place, the two things jostled together, making the banana screech and shriek the whole way.

Dawn and Darby were already standing next to the cannon when I arrived.

"What's that racket?" Dawn asked, looking around.

"Mom's gift!" I said proudly. I pulled out the Screaming Banana and showed them. "See? It will make her laugh. Mom needs to laugh more."

"No offense, Delaney, but it will probably give her headaches," Dawn said. She reached down and picked up a bag at her feet. "Look what I got." Inside was a small birdhouse shaped like an old red barn. "That way she can look at birds and it will make her feel calm. Mom needs to feel calmer."

"But how will she see them? All of our trees are far away from the house, and birds won't nest on the porch with Quincy sleeping there," Darby pointed out.

"Guess that means we should go for the banana," I said.

"Actually, I think I found something for her," Darby said with a big smile. She picked up a box and held it out for us to see. Inside were cookie cutters in different flower shapes. "There's even a lily!"

"That's nice, Darby," I said, "but . . . remember our gift last year?" Last Christmas we'd found a really cool baking set that lets you make star-shaped cookies and cakes in the shape of the American flag. Only Mom must have had a busy year, because it was still in the cupboard in its box.

"Oh. Yeah." Darby looked so crestfallen, I felt awful for having reminded her.

"Well, that's just dandy," Dawn grumbled. "Now we have three useless gifts."

"I guess we should split up and return them," I said.

"No," Darby said. "Let's walk around and think about it some more. We've already looked everywhere, so one of these will have to do, right?"

We agreed she was right. And anyway, we always like strolling through town this time of year. Johnson City is always done up pretty around the holidays, with long strands of lights edging the limestone brick courthouse and hanging in strands from its roof, not to mention the millions of lights just down the road in the trees of the Pedernales Electric Co-op property. There was even a wreath hanging on the World War II cannon beside us. The town is especially pretty at night — like a twinkly fairyland. But it's nice in the daytime, too.

Since I walked fast and bouncy, the Screaming Banana kept going off, so Darby suggested that she carry my bag. And Dawn put Darby's gift in her own bag. That allowed me to swing my arms and grab porch posts, so I could whirl around them. The more I move, the better I think, and I was hoping to think of ways to convince them that the Screaming Banana was the best gift option for Mom.

Just then, someone caught my eye. I'm not sure what it was that made this person stand out. Perhaps the color? Out on the square, there was lots of red and green and white, but this person was all in black — black leather coat, black skirt, black ripped stockings, and black pirate boots with big buckles on them. Plus, everyone else was bustling about in a hurry, but this person was slouched on the courthouse steps, looking bored. In any case, I recognized her right away.

"Bree! Bree! Bree!" I quickly spun around, jumped up and down, and started waving my arms. A couple of people passing nearby made mad faces at me. Dawn and Darby looked startled, too.

I zoomed across the lawn toward her.

"Hey, Delaney." Bree smiled as I ran up. Well, not exactly. Bree acts like she's bored with everything all the time, so instead of smiling she does this thing where her face goes smooth.

Bree likes to wear thick black eyeliner like an ancient Egyptian, and her hair was now red, but not like ours. While ours is kind of blondish-brownish red and we usually wear braids, Bree's hair had been dyed the color of ketchup and she keeps it really messy. But if you look past all the makeup and wild hair and ripped stockings, you'll notice that she has a delicate face, with big sparkly blue eyes and round cheeks like the top of a valentine.

She kind of reminds me of a doll that's been colored on and kicked around.

Bree and I got to be pretty good pals during the Almost Wedding last summer. She was one of the bridesmaids, but she helped us pull off our plan to delay the wedding. I think she did it because she was bored and mad about having to be a bridesmaid, but also because — like us — she could tell that Lily wasn't happy and was about to make a big mistake.

"What are you three up to?" she asked as Dawn and Darby caught up with us.

"Christmas shopping," I said. "What about you?"

"Looking for a job."

I nodded, but actually it didn't seem like Bree was looking for a job. She was just sitting there.

"What kind of a job are you looking for?" Dawn asked.

She shrugged. "I don't know. Something reasonable. I was working at the donut place, but they were ridiculous. They wanted me to be there at seven in the morning and wear a brown polyester uniform. With a hat!" She shut her eyes and a shiver went through her. "Anyway, I had to quit, of course. But now I'm sick of not having any money."

"What are you going to do?" Darby asked.

"Beats me," Bree said, tugging at a loose thread in her stockings. "I've been looking around town but haven't found anything."

"Yeah, we know what you mean," Dawn said. "We've been buying Christmas gifts for our mom but nothing seems right."

"Do you have any suggestions?" Darby asked Bree.

"Not a single one," Bree said. "Do you have any suggestions where I might find a job?"

Dawn, Darby, and I all shook our heads.

Bree pulled out a scrap of paper and a pen from her black messenger bag. "Tell you what," she said, writing on the shred of paper. "Here's my cell number. If you hear of any brilliant job opportunities, give me a call. And if you give me your number, I'll call you if I think of any splendid mom gifts."

We agreed that this sounded like a fair trade. Dawn took the piece of paper, and I told Bree the number to Mom's house so she could enter it into her phone.

"If we aren't there it means we're out trying to help the Neighbors or picking up Mom and Lily from the airport," Dawn said.

"That reminds me. I saw that guy a minute ago. The

one you wanted your sister to get back together with at the wedding," Bree said.

"You mean Alex?" I asked. "You saw him? Where?"

"He passed by me about twenty minutes ago. Looked like he was in a hurry, too." She stood and shouldered her messenger bag. "Well, I'd better keep looking. See ya."

I got up on my tiptoes and scanned all the people I could see. But none of them were Alex. Then I turned the opposite direction . . . and there he was, on the other side of Cypress Street!

I ran to the edge of the courthouse lawn, looked both ways twice, and zoomed across the road toward him.

"Alex! Alex, Alex, Alex!" I shouted while jumping up and down. Again, a couple of people close to me looked annoyed. "Sorry," I said to them.

Finally, the three of us caught up to him.

"Hey!" I said. "What are you up to?"

"Hi . . ." he said, stretching out the word as he glanced at each one of us. Alex had a strange look on his face. His eyes were all big and his eyebrows were S-shaped and he was holding his coat tight as if he were cold.

"Do you feel all right?" Darby asked.

"Actually, um . . . I have to run," he said. "Good seeing you!" And then he took off.

Usually when people say they have to run it just means they don't have much time to chat. But Alex actually sprinted down the street as if he were in a race, or he'd just remembered he left the bathwater running.

"What was that?" Dawn asked.

"Is he mad at us?" Darby asked.

I watched the back of Alex's head bobbing down the sidewalk. Eventually, he took a left and disappeared. I wasn't even sure what to think. It seemed like Alex didn't want to talk to us, but I had no idea why.

"What is it with Christmas?" I wondered aloud. "It makes adults act so weird."

CHAPTER ELEVEN

Probable Cause

Dawn

You know that saying "My patience has worn thin"? I never really understood it until now. But with the pageant fiasco and not finding the Santa-napper and Quincy's destruction of Dad's sofa and getting swindled out of four days with Lily and not being able to find the right gift for Mom . . . Well, my patience did feel like one of those sheets that has been through the washer and dryer so many times, it ends up frayed and see-through and irregularly shaped.

After Alex acted like he wanted nothing to do with us, we decided to head back home. We had to check on Quincy and make sure he hadn't torn anything up, and we needed to hide the tinsel tree we got for Dad before he came home. But mostly, we'd just lost heart. In the meantime, we decided to hold on to the not-quite-right gifts until we figured out what we'd give Mom.

Delaney was being a big worrywart.

"What happens if we never find the ideal present for Mom?" she asked.

"We will. Mom doesn't come home until tomorrow night. And then we have a couple more days after that until Christmas. We'll have time to make up our minds," I said.

"But what if we decide she won't like any of these and we don't get any new ideas and then we're out of places to shop?"

"We'll come up with something."

"But what if —"

"Ding-dang it, Delaney!" I hollered. "Have a little faith!"

"I'm sorry," she said. And she did have a mighty sorrowful look on her face. It made me feel like a meanie.

"We just need to stay calm," Darby said. "The only thing we have to fear is fear itself."

We got to the part of the road where there isn't a sidewalk and the grassy part between people's fences and the asphalt is pretty narrow. Lily taught us to walk single file when we walk down this stretch, so we automatically got in a line. Delaney was in front, followed by Darby, and then me.

Eventually, we rounded a bend and there was the Neighbors' house up ahead. Our house's roof, just across the street, was visible above the trees.

Mr. Neighbor was on his front porch, reading. When he saw us, he lifted his hand in a wave and shouted, "Make way for ducklings!"

He says that every time he sees us walking past. It's like a joke, only jokes are supposed to be a surprise. If you know someone is going to say something, how can it be funny? But we still like it and we'd probably be disappointed if he didn't say it. So I guess it's more like an inside joke than a funny ha-ha joke.

"Hi, Mr. Neighbor," we greeted him.

Delaney leaned over the top of the fence. "Has there been any progress with the case?"

"Did you find St. Nick?" Darby asked.

"Did they catch the offender?" I asked.

Mr. Neighbor walked over to us, shaking his head. "I'm afraid not. But I do appreciate your concern."

"Stuff like that shouldn't happen — especially during Christmas," I grumbled.

"I agree," Mr. Neighbor said. "And that's almost exactly what your friend said this morning."

I tilted my head, wondering. "Which friend?"

"I can't recall his name. It was the boy who came by on his new bicycle that day we were waiting for your father."

Darby, Delaney, and I made big, surprised eyes. "Lucas Westbrook?" Delaney asked.

Mr. Neighbor nodded. "That's the one. He stopped by to say he'd heard about my St. Nick going missing and that he was sorry."

I tilted my head the other direction, thinking hard. Something wasn't right. "But . . . how did he know it was missing? Darby, did you tell him?"

Darby shook her head.

"Did you, Delaney?"

"No."

Suddenly, my brain seized up with a thought — a big, bold thought that took over everything and kicked all other notions out of my head. I quickly shoved my shopping bag into Delaney's hands and started trotting down the road speedy quick. As I went, I talked over my shoulder in that chattering way that Delaney uses all the time: "Thanks-Mr.-Neighbor-we'll-see-you-later-give-our-best-to-Mrs.-Neighbor-we'll-talk-with-you-soon!"

I could hear Darby and Delaney running after me — not them, exactly, but that blasted Screaming Banana. I was several yards away before they caught up with me.

"Dawn! You went past our house. What's going on?" Delaney asked.

"Lucas Westbrook!" I replied.

"What about him?"

"I have to stop that spoiled son of a spoiler!" I said a little breathlessly. "I'm going to pick him up and shake him until that Santa falls out of him!"

"What are you talking about?" Darby asked. "You're acting all deranged again." Which was a silly thing to say since she was the one with the screeching shopping bag.

Delaney zoomed in front of me and stood with her right hand on her hip and her left arm straight out in front of her in a HALT sign.

I stopped right before we collided.

"Don't you get it?" I said. I was irritated that they stopped me and even more irritated that I had to explain something so obvious. "If Lucas knew that the Santa was missing, but none of us told him, that means he's the one who took it!"

Darby and Delaney traded shocked expressions.

"Ms. Woolcott did say it was probably kids playing a prank," Delaney said.

"And he knew about the Santa," I reminded them. "We saw him admire it that day we were waiting for Dad."

"But wait a minute. Let's stop and think," said Darby, who's always the boring voice of reason. "Why would Lucas take it? He already has everything in the world."

"He didn't have a hundred-year-old Santa candy dispenser," I pointed out.

"Maybe when he saw it, it drove him bonkers that he didn't have one," Delaney said, boinging on her toes. "Then he came back during the night and took it!"

"Well . . . he did hear us say it was invaluable," Darby said. She finally seemed to be considering the possibility that Lucas was the Santa-napper.

"There's really only one way to find out if he's guilty," I said. "We need to confront him."

Darby and Delaney agreed, and we walked four more blocks down to Lucas's house.

The Westbrook house isn't real old like ours. It's brick instead of wood and is painted white with black shutters.

I'll admit, it makes me envious that he gets to live in a stately white house. Ours is a yellowy cream color, like butter, but it does have white trim. Inside, in the front part of Lucas's house, the ceilings are so high your voice echoes, and if you wear hard shoes, they tap on the shiny stone floor. Upstairs, in the back part of the house, Lucas has not one, but three whole rooms — a game room, a playroom, and his bedroom, all full of stuff. And he doesn't have to share with anyone, since he's an only child.

Once, we played hide-and-seek and lost Darby. She had crawled up inside the nose of his rocket fort and fell asleep while waiting for us to find her. It took over an hour before someone thought to peek inside that thing.

That was three years ago. For some reason, we didn't hang out with Lucas as much after we turned ten.

Lucas answered the door when we rang the bell.

"Hey!" he said. "Come on in. I want to show you my new present."

Delaney and I rolled our eyes at each other as we followed him inside, wiping our feet carefully and setting our bags by the door. I imagine Lucas's family will soon run out of things to give him. When that happens they'll probably start buying him clouds and mountains and towns and a real train to get him there.

It turned out to be an air hockey table, with lights and sound effects. A giant red bow had been taped beside the electronic scoreboard.

"My dad was playing against me this morning, but he had to go to work," he said. "Want to play? I beat my dad ten to seven."

"Not right now." I glanced back at Darby and Delaney, who were standing right behind me, one on either side. We looked like a sheriff and two deputies. Or a super-hero and two sidekicks. Or maybe a rock star and two backup singers. I supposed it didn't matter what we resembled as long as he could tell we meant business. "Actually, Lucas, we're not here to hang out. We just need to ask you a few questions."

"Oh."

I studied Lucas's demeanor carefully. He did seem to act differently all of a sudden. His shoulders sagged and his expression went droopy. Looked like guilt to me.

I didn't waste any time. "Lucas Westbrook, where were you two evenings ago?"

His eyebrows zoomed to the top of his head. "Out riding my new bike. You saw me."

"I mean after that. When it was dark."

"I was sleeping. And eating supper," he said. "I mean, I was eating supper and then sleeping."

"Hmm . . ." I tapped my chin and stared hard at him. "Having a hard time keeping your story straight, huh?"

Lucas tilted his head. "What do you mean?"

"I mean, it seems like there was plenty of time to do other things that night — things you didn't bother to mention. What do you have to say to that?"

"Well . . . yeah." Lucas looked down at the floor. "I didn't think I should bring up going to the bathroom."

I took a step forward and hollered, "Come out with it, Lucas! Why did you steal the Neighbors' Santa?"

"What?" Lucas's mouth hung open for a couple of seconds. "Why would I steal the Santa?"

"Why indeed?" I crossed my arms over my chest and narrowed my eyes at him.

Lucas didn't seem to understand what I was asking. Honestly, I wasn't sure, either. All I know is that in the TV detective shows, when a suspect asks a question they turn it around on him. Usually, the suspect can't explain himself and confesses. But Lucas just bunched up his face in a confused look.

"Huh?" he said.

Delaney stepped forward on my left. "Lucas Westbrook, did you or did you not stop by the Neighbors' house earlier today and ask about the missing Santa?" she asked. She rested her fists on her hips, as if daring him to lie.

"I did," he said. "So what?"

Darby stepped forward on my right. "So how did you know the Santa was missing?" She lifted her chin in a challenging way. She didn't look as fierce as Delaney, but she was trying — I could tell. I was proud of her for that.

Lucas just stared back at her with that same bumfuzzled expression on his face. "Your neighbor told me," he said.

"Ha!" I exclaimed, pointing my finger at him. "We know for a fact that he didn't. Mr. Neighbor said he had no idea how you knew the Santa was stolen." I couldn't help smiling. This was it. We'd caught the Santa-napper!

"Not Mr. Neighbor. Your other neighbor. I forget her name. The one with the puffed-out hair." Lucas held his hands two inches away from his head to demonstrate.

"Ms. Woolcott?" Darby asked.

He nodded. "Yes, that's her," he said. "I was going past on my new skateboard to see if you guys were home and

131

she told me the Santa had been stolen. I was sorry to hear it. Mr. Neighbor is really nice."

All I could say was, "Oh."

Darby, Delaney, and I glanced at each other, unsure what to do next. I felt awful foolish. I was disappointed in myself for not considering Ms. Woolcott as a source, and I was frustrated that we hadn't caught the culprit after all.

Lucas didn't seem all that upset, though. He just perked up and patted the table beside him. "So do you want to play some air hockey?"

"No, thanks," I said. "We need to get back home and check on our dog."

"Yeah, last time we left him for a long while, he ate a couch," Delaney said.

Lucas's eyes popped open wide. "Whoa."

"Sorry about interrogating you, Lucas," Darby said. "That was rude of us."

"That's okay. You guys can come over anytime."

We followed him downstairs and gathered our bags. Then we each shook his hand and agreed to keep him posted on the investigation.

"See you at the pageant," he said. He gave a final wave and shut the big, heavy door.

I marched down the walkway to the sidewalk and started pacing up and down in front of the Westbrook house, shaking my head and muttering.

"We might be giving up too easily," I said. "I don't know if I'm ready to eliminate Lucas as a suspect. Did you see all that stuff in there? What if he has the Santa hidden away in a safe or a treasure chest? And we still need to verify his story. I mean, would Ms. Woolcott actually take the time to tell him about the Santa-napping?"

Delaney nodded. "Of course she would. She loves telling people things she knows about other people."

"And Lucas has always had lots of stuff, but he's never stolen anything. Not that we know of," Darby said. She leaned forward to stare into my eyes. "You don't actually think we should continue to investigate him, do you?" There were squiggles of worry on her brow.

"Yes! Maybe?" I let out a grunt and stamped my sneaker against the sidewalk. "I have no idea. I just want something to go right. You know?"

"We know," Delaney said.

"We feel the same way," Darby said.

With her free arm she grabbed my hand and Delaney grabbed my other one and we stayed like that all the way home. It wasn't easy — especially on the narrow stretches, and with that ridiculous fruit toy yelling the whole way — but it helped.

It was like holding on to the safety rail while going down a steep staircase. I felt steady and upright, and I knew I could keep going.

CHAPTER TWELVE

Domestic Tranquility

Darby

My favorite thing to do at Christmastime is lie under the Christmas tree with all the lights off except for the colored, blinking strands on the tree and watch the patterns they make on the ceiling. It always seems magical — as if I stepped inside a kaleidoscope — and I can feel the joy and peace and merriment that everyone sings about during the holidays.

But when we came home after confronting Lucas, I didn't feel those things. I lay there and watched the blue, green, gold, and red dance on the ceiling, and I waited for those happy feelings to spring up inside me. Only they didn't. All I could do was fret and feel guilty.

The Neighbors have been like grandparents to us, and it makes me want to go all Dawn-like on whoever took the St. Nick candy container. But the worst of it is, I hate thinking that someone we know, maybe even another neighbor, might have done such a thing. I didn't like the thought that someone in our town — maybe someone on our block, or someone we went to church with — might have taken Mr. Neighbor's family heirloom. I don't like looking at people we've known our whole lives and wondering if they could have done something so mean. And if we ever find out who it is, the first thing I'll do is ask them why. Because I need to understand their reasons, even if I don't agree with them. Otherwise the world doesn't make sense.

"So . . . what's supposed to happen?" Dawn asked beside me.

The three of us had felt so icky after we grilled Lucas that afternoon, and after the fiasco of gift shopping, that I told them about my lying-under-the-tree trick. Apparently, it wasn't working on them, either.

"If you focus on the patterns, you forget everything and just feel peaceful and content," I explained. "Do you feel anything?"

"Well . . . the floor hurts my back," Dawn said. "It's itchy, too, from all the needles that have fallen off the tree. That's pretty much all I'm feeling."

"I like it better *this* way," Delaney was saying. After about two minutes, she had given up lying under the tree and was now spinning around while staring at the lights on the ceiling. "This way makes the designs swirl."

"If you knock over this tree, Delaney, I won't be responsible for what I do to you," Dawn warned as she slid out from under the tree and got to her feet. "We don't need anything else to go wrong."

"Fine." Delaney stopped spinning, staggered backward a couple of steps, and plunked down on the sofa. She looked a little cross-eyed.

I stood and brushed the needles off my clothes. "Well, that was a bust. Sorry it didn't help."

Dawn reached over and patted my arm. "It's all right. It was nice of you to suggest your weird habit to us."

"And I got to invent a colorful swirly spin," Delaney said.

We heard the creak of the swinging kitchen door and Dad poked his head out. "Hey, girls, I thought you said that there was bread."

"There is," I said. "Whole wheat and that seedy kind that Lily likes. Mom keeps it in the freezer so that it doesn't get moldy."

"I see. But, um . . . what about when you want to eat it?"

"Toaster. Lowest setting," Dawn said.

"Gotcha." Dad saluted us with the spatula. "Thanks, girls!"

The swinging door groaned again as he went back through to the kitchen. Soon we could hear him whistling "Wonderful Christmastime" as he rummaged through the freezer.

At least Dad was in a happy mood. He'd gotten good news today, so we were celebrating with his famous BLTs for dinner.

As soon as he'd arrived home from work he told us he had a chance to land a major deal. A surgeon he'd been visiting for months and months finally called and told him to be in Houston two days from now at five in the morning, and to bring his knee parts for an operation they had scheduled. Apparently, if Dad won an account with this surgery center, he would earn more money overall — maybe even enough to move into a bigger apartment. He'd been wanting that for a while.

Since Dad had good news and Mom and Lily would be back the next evening, we knew we shouldn't be feeling so gloomy. But we did. Even Delaney, with all her spinning and bouncing, was kind of sluggish.

"I just want to feel Christmas-y. That's all," Dawn mumbled as she flopped onto the couch.

"We could sing," Delaney suggested. "Or we could watch Charlie Brown again."

Dawn shook her head. "Those things don't last," she said. "We need something that will lift our spirits and keep them up."

As I lay sideways across the armchair and ruminated, I realized that the time I felt the most Christmas-y over the past few days was when I was sitting on the Neighbors' porch. It was cozy and welcoming and made me feel at home — even though it was someone else's home.

That gave me an idea.

"I know what we should do," I said. "We should decorate our porch."

"Why?" Delaney asked.

"Because then other people can see the decorations and it will feel like we're sharing," I said. "Right now all of our decorations are inside."

"I . . . guess I understand what you mean?" Dawn said slowly.

Delaney started bouncing on her toes. "And we can set up Dad's tree!"

I agreed that this was a terrific plan. And Dawn said it was better than lying on a hard floor. So while Dad made BLTs and tomato soup for dinner, we quietly gathered up the extra tinsel garlands, candy canes, and bows, along with Dad's tree, and went out onto the porch.

First we wove the silver tinsel garland around the porch railing. It didn't make it all the way from one end to the other, but it almost did. Then we hung candy canes on the garland and tied bows to the porch posts. When we were done, we stepped into the center of the yard to admire our work.

"You're right," Dawn said. "It does make things feel better. I don't know why, but it does."

"And it will make other people smile," Delaney said, bouncing happily.

Even Quincy was in a merry mood. He had found one of his old rawhides and was rolling around, making joyful snorts and grunts.

Next we set up Dad's tree in the corner of the porch. We figured it would be more help to him and an even bigger surprise if we decorated it ourselves. Then he could take it with him tomorrow and have some Christmas cheer in the apartment.

We had found a box of ornaments in the hall closet that Mom must have forgotten about. Most of them we made when we were little — like the pinecone owls they had us put together in Sunday school. They don't much look like owls anymore, since the triangular pieces we used for the beak, wings, and top of the head fell off. Basically, they're just pinecones with bird feet and googly eyes. There's also the snowman ornament I made in second grade. I remember Frank Janecek had used up all the black paint on his Batman ornament, so I used blue for the snowman's eyes and red for the coal buttons on his middle. Unfortunately, the red paint was a little runny, so it ended up looking like my snowman had three major wounds instead of buttons.

The George Globes were in the box, too. George Globes were Dawn's creation back when we were five. We'd been making ornaments by sticking small photos inside clear plastic balls with multicolored confetti to make it festive. We'd made one using a picture of each member of the family, including one of Quincy as a puppy, so we had seven in all. Then Dawn decided to make one for George Washington, her favorite president. Only we didn't have a photo of George Washington. So instead, she took dollar bills out of our piggy bank and cut his face out. Mom was a little mad about that. Dad was, too, although he said he was grateful she didn't worship Ben Franklin.

Anyway, we stuck the snowman, a couple of the owls, and the George Globes on Dad's new tree, along with a couple of leftover candy canes, and put a bow on top. It didn't look like your typical Christmas tree at all, but it looked nice. It looked like . . . our family. And we were happy that Dad would have mementos of when he used to live here.

Already we felt better.

From inside the house we could hear Dad calling out to us.

"Quick!" Dawn said. "Let's get over by the decorations."

We stood in a line and waited eagerly. Delaney bounced, I laughed, and Dawn made a high-pitched whinny sound in her throat.

A few seconds later, Dad opened the front door. "Girls, wash up and come to —"

"Surprise!" we shouted together.

"What in the world?" he exclaimed. He stepped onto the porch and glanced all around. "What have you three been up to?"

"We decorated!" I said. "The porch is for everyone. Neighbors and passersby can enjoy it, too."

"And the tree is for you," Delaney said. "You get to take it with you tomorrow. That way you can have Christmas cheer at your barren apartment."

"You haven't had time to decorate, so we did some for you," Dawn said.

Dad stepped closer to the tree. "Oh, look! It's the George Globes! And Survivor Snowman! I'd almost forgotten about those guys. And the . . . the . . . what are those things again?"

"Owls," Dawn said.

"Right. Girls, this is so . . . so . . . ." He swallowed and his eyes blinked hard a few times. "It's very thoughtful of you. Thank you," he finished, his voice kind of low and scratchy.

It felt like a balloon was swelling inside my chest, making me floaty. Dawn said we needed a win, and now we had one. Finally, something had gone right.

"All right." Dad clapped his hands together. "Let's have dinner, clean the kitchen, make cocoa, and come right back out here to admire your work. Should we eat in the kitchen or dining room?"

"Kitchen!" the three of us said at the same time.

In our house we have two places to eat. We have a big formal dining room table and a smaller one in the kitchen by the window. Usually, we eat in the kitchen when it's just family because it's easier. Also because the dining room one is almost always covered with stuff like puzzles or a Monopoly game or our homemade diorama of the Treaty of Ghent.

"Kitchen it is," Dad said as we all headed back inside. "You guys wash up. I need to turn off the stove before the soup overcooks." He zipped off toward the kitchen. As soon as he pushed through the swinging door, we heard a buzzing sound coming from the coffee table.

"Dad, your phone is ringing!" Dawn called out to him.

"Can you check it?" he called back.

Delaney was closest. "It's Mom!" she said, scooping it up.

"Don't tell her about the porch, okay?" I whispered. "Let it be a surprise?"

Delaney nodded.

I skipped toward the bathroom, humming a made-up

melody. I couldn't believe I'd come up with a plan that worked so well.

Before I got to the end of the hall, I turned and glimpsed the Christmas tree in the back corner of the living room. The lights seemed to be winking at me.

I winked back.

CHAPTER THIRTEEN

Cold War

Delaney

Hi, Mom. How's Boston? How's Aunt Jane? Did Lily see those colleges yet? Did she like them? I kind of hope she didn't. I think she should go someplace closer."

"This is Lily," came Lily's voice over the phone. "Mom's busy. Is this Delaney?"

I gulped. "Yes. Sorry I said all that stuff about the library schools. I didn't mean it."

"It's all right. Listen, there's been some big changes here because of the snow. We need to talk to Dad."

"It's snowing in Boston?" I felt a little jealous. "Wow. I'd love it if it snowed here — real snow and not just the paltry layer we usually get. We could make snow angels and snowmen and I could run around trying to catch snowflakes on my tongue. Mrs. Neighbor even told me she has a recipe that lets you make ice cream out of snow. Can you bring some snow back for us? Maybe in a cooler?"

"It's actually not as nice as it sounds," Lily said. "It's snowing so much that they've canceled all flights."

"You mean . . . none of the planes can leave? Does that mean your plane, too?"

"I'm afraid so. It looks like we're going to have to stay here at least one more day — maybe longer. Who knows how long it will take for the airport to sort out all the people stranded here?"

A prickly sensation swept over me, as if I were cold. "But . . . but . . . it's only three days until Christmas! Will you be back in time?"

"I don't know. I hope so. Mom's on the computer now, looking at other options."

Dawn and Darby were back from washing up and were now standing right in front of me with matching expressions. Their mouths were slightly open in surprise and their eyes were saggy in a sad look. They could tell something was wrong.

"Mom's back. She said she needs to talk to Dad about all this," Lily said. "Can you hand the phone over?"

"Okay," I said. My voice was low and wobbly. It almost sounded like someone else.

I headed into the kitchen with Dawn and Darby trotting along behind me. Dad was singing "Run Run Rudolph" while ladling soup into four bowls.

I held out his cell phone. "Mom needs to talk to you," I said. "It's important."

As soon as he took it, I ran back into the living room and started pacing around. Dawn and Darby trotted right back after me.

"I wish you'd be still and tell us what's going on," Dawn said.

"Just hang on a sec," I said, breaking into a slight jog. I didn't want to tell them. I didn't want to say it out loud. And when I'm upset, it helps to move around. I was hoping a few laps around the sofa would get me calmed down enough to share the bad news.

"Delaney, please stop," Darby said. "Delaney?"

"Just one more circle," I said. I came around the end of the couch and suddenly there was Dawn standing in front of me. All I could see were points — the sharp elbows of her crossed arms and the tip of her chin as she raised her head defiantly. It looked hazardous. So I came to an abrupt halt and wavered a bit on my feet.

"Tell us!" she commanded.

"Mom and Lily might not make it back in time for Christmas," I said. I told them what Lily had said about the snowstorm and the airlines being backed up.

"But how can we have Christmas without them?" Darby asked.

Dawn and I shrugged. Soon we were all pacing around the couch — Quincy, too. He'd given up on his rawhide and was trotting after us, whimpering a little. It was like he understood.

Darby veered away after a couple of laps and turned on the TV. She found our weather channel, where a big radar image filled the screen. Sure enough, in the upper-right corner, covering most of New England, was a massive purple blotch with the words WINTER STORM WARNING above it. She plunked down in front of the set and gaped at the awful sight. Dawn and I sat on either side of her.

"It looks horrible," Dawn said.

"It's huge," Darby said.

"It's ruining everything!" I said.

A woman's voice on the TV said they would now show "future animation." As the clock at the top of the screen went forward really fast, the colors on the map moved — except for the snowstorm over Massachusetts and the

149

surrounding states. The big purple blob changed shape, but it didn't go away.

"I don't care about a zip line," Darby said. "Now I just want Mom and Lily back."

"Me, too," I said. "I can get my mynah bird some other time. Birds are nice and chattery and dinosaur-like, but family is most important."

Darby and I looked over at Dawn. She scowled at the TV. "I could sure use a megaphone," she said.

"Dawn!" Darby looked shocked.

"Fine. I admit it. I want Mom and Lily home more than I want my present." Dawn relented. "Stupid storm."

"I feel like Christmas hates us this year," Darby said in a whimpery voice.

I completely agreed, and Dawn must have, too. We each leaned toward Darby until our heads touched hers and threw our arms around her shoulders.

Just then, we heard the *crick-crick-crick-crick* sound of the kitchen door slowly opening, and Dad trudged into the living room, holding his phone to his ear. We stood up expectantly, and Dawn turned off the TV.

"Yes, I'm sorry, too. All we can do is wait and see," Dad was saying. His posture was slumpy and his words came out low and empty-sounding. It was the exact opposite of the singing, whistling Dad we'd had just a few minutes before.

"Okay. Keep us posted. Be safe. Bye." Dad turned off his phone and let out the longest sigh I've ever heard.

"Is Christmas canceled?" Dawn asked. She looked like she might cry.

"Are they going to be okay?" Darby asked. She was already crying a little bit.

"What if the weather stays bad and they have to live in Boston all winter?" I asked. I wasn't crying, but my voice was all crackly and quivery.

Quincy made one of his worried-sounding groans and flopped across Darby's feet.

"Hey, whoa, it's okay," Dad said. "Everything's going to be all right."

We didn't believe him and it showed on our faces. Even Quincy continued to bellyache.

"We will still have Christmas, even if they don't make it back in time," Dad said.

Darby made a squeaky noise.

"All it would mean is that Christmas would be extra long this year," Dad went on. "You'd celebrate on the actual day and again when Lily and your mom get back."

He waited for us to say something, but all we could do was moan along with Quincy.

Finally, he blew out his breath, plopped down into the armchair, and said, "Yeah, it's a real lousy turn of events. There's just no denying it."

Here's a funny thing. The minute Dad agreed that it was a crummy situation, we stopped whining.

"It'll be all right," Darby said.

"Yeah, we can have Christmas any old time," Dawn said.

"We should focus on the positive," I said. "Like . . . your deal at the Houston hospital. That's a good thing, right?"

Dad only looked sadder. He rested his elbows on his knees and slouched forward, his hands making a little resting cup for his forehead. "I'll probably have to cancel that."

"But why?" I asked.

"Because there's no way I'm leaving you girls alone overnight," he said.

"But we can take care of ourselves!" Dawn said. Darby and I added *yeahs*.

Dad raised his head and shook it over and over. "It's not possible."

"Yes, it is." Dawn huffed up and crossed her arms. "You just don't trust us."

"It's not for long," Darby said.

"It would be easy," I said.

"It would be neglectful, and probably illegal," Dad said.

"Oh." We all fell silent. We wanted our dad to land the account, but we didn't want him to become an outlaw.

The lights were still dimmed from when we lay beneath the tree to see the patterns on the ceiling, and the sun had gone down. Everything had turned some shade of gray and was completely still — even me. It would have felt gloomy in the shadows and silence, but in the corner, the Christmas tree sparkled. Just looking at it made me feel hopeful on the inside.

I don't know how long we were quiet like that, but my mind started considering the lights. I thought about the Wise Men following the bright star in the sky and how that light had given them hope. I thought about trying to catch fireflies on the lawn with my sisters in the summer. I thought about how we say things like "light at the end of the tunnel" or "the future looks bright" or that someone's face "lights up." And I thought about how having a good idea is like a lightbulb going off over someone's head.

And then I got a lightbulb over *my* head.

"Dad, what if you hired a babysitter for us?" I asked.

Dawn looked daggers at me. "That's a terrible idea," she said. "We're too old for babysitters."

"Do you mean Mr. and Mrs. Neighbor?" Darby asked.

"Not Ms. Woolcott!" Dawn said with a gasp.

I shook my head. "I mean Bree."

CHAPTER FOURTEEN

Security Breach

Dawn

I guess if you are too old for a babysitter, but you still have to have one because of a stupid law, then having someone like Bree is a good compromise.

Bree is seventeen, so she's old enough to babysit but young enough to want to have fun while doing it. And she thinks we're "splendid." She uses that word a lot because she wants to go to England someday and she says that's what everyone says there.

Anyway, Dad was pretty desperate for help, so that also worked in our favor. We promised we'd be on our best behavior and told him he could check in with us as often as he wanted. And Darby suggested he call the Neighbors or Ms. Woolcott and ask them to regularly make sure the house was still standing. He finally agreed and called the number Bree had given us. Bree's only concern was how early she'd have to arrive. When Dad said, "Nine in the morning," she agreed to take the job.

At two minutes past nine we heard her boots clomping up our porch steps. Bree rapped a rhythm on our door, and Dad carefully opened it up while balancing his two duffel bags and a thermos of coffee.

"Bree! Thanks so much for coming," he said. "There's a list of important numbers on the counter and I have your number on my phone. I also left money for food and anything else you might need. I'll check in fairly regularly, but of course you can contact me or anyone on the list if you need something. Sound okay?"

"Sure," she said.

"When I need to talk to the girls, I'll call their mom's office phone and you'll see my number pop up. Feel free to ignore it otherwise," he said.

He probably added that last part because Mrs. Higginbotham kept leaving messages suggesting cookie recipes for Mom.

"Sounds good," Bree said.

"You girls behave," Dad said to us. We all swarmed around him, giving him hugs. "Gotta go now, sweetheart.

I'm running late," he said when Darby wouldn't let go of him. As soon as she stepped back he blew us kisses and ran out the door. A few seconds later we could hear his Volkswagen bus chugging down the driveway and onto the street.

"Wow," Bree said, staring after him. "That dude seems stressed."

"He's trying to land a big client," Delaney explained.

"That way he can afford a bigger place," Darby said.

"And a new couch," I added.

Bree set down a big black bag and Quincy started sniffing all over it. "So what happened to y'all's house?" she asked, motioning with her thumb toward the porch behind her.

"We decorated yesterday," I explained. "Isn't it splendid?"

Bree shrugged. "I guess. Most people don't go for a ripped-up look the way I do, but bully for you for defying the norm."

"Ripped-up look?" Darby repeated.

The three of us exchanged quick, worried glances and then rushed past Bree out the door. Quincy followed close behind, thinking it was playtime. Our stockinged feet skidded to a stop on the porch.

All of our decorations were wrecked. The tinsel garland was mostly gone — only two shredded pieces hung limply from the railing. One of the bows was missing, and the two that remained were unraveled and crooked. Scattered all over the porch were pinecone owls, some with missing eyeballs or feet, and a couple of George Globes. We followed the trail to the back corner, where Dad's tree lay on its side. Darby's bloody-looking snowman stuck out from underneath it.

It was awful — like the set of a Christmas horror movie. All we could do was wander about, gasping and yelping at every casualty. Quincy trotted a twisty path around the porch, sniffing at everything and making low, growly whines.

"I'm guessing you didn't want it to look like this," Bree said, sitting on the porch swing.

I narrowed my eyes at her. "Of course not."

"So what happened?" she asked.

"It's the Santa-napper! He attacked our house!" Delaney exclaimed.

"That . . . that . . . monster!" Darby wailed, then knelt down and freed poor Survivor Snowman. She tried to stand Dad's tree back up, but all the branches were bent on one side, so it just kept toppling over again.

"What Santa-napper?" Bree asked.

We filled her in on the whole saga while we picked up the mess and straightened out Dad's tree so that it would stay upright. It took a while, because we were so upset. None of us wanted to cry in front of Bree, but I kept grunting and muttering, and Delaney kept running laps around the house, saying she was checking the yard for missing ornaments. Darby turned her head away from us and wouldn't talk at all. Occasionally, we'd hear a sniffling sound or a hiccup.

The more I worked, and the more I saw how upset my sisters were, the angrier I got. It was awful enough that this Scrooge person had messed with our neighbors and friends, but now he was messing with my family. Someone had actually come onto our porch while we were sleeping and done something terrible!

If I were already president, I'd declare war on him.

"I don't understand," Bree said after we finished telling her the whole sorry story. "Why would this person wreck your porch?"

"Yeah, I don't get it, either," Delaney said, panting a little from her latest lap. "We didn't have anything priceless, like the Neighbors."

"I don't know, but if I ever find this guy," I said, "I'm going to . . . hang him by our chimney — without care!"

I was holding a George Globe in my hand and had to fight the urge to smash it against the wall.

I wondered if I'd ever feel the same pride for our town that I used to. I wondered if I would ever love Christmas again.

I had to do something to let go of the angry feelings, so I decided to head upstairs and pound a pillow. "Excuse me," I mumbled, and headed inside.

As soon as I stepped through the door, I could hear the phone ringing in Mom's office. I went in to see if it was Mrs. Higginbotham — I almost hoped it was so I could let out my anger on her — and saw that it was coming from Mom's cell phone. "Hello?" I said, picking up.

"Hi, who is this? Dawn?"

"Yep."

"Is your dad there? I can't reach him on his cell."

"He left to go out of town for a couple of days. He's driving, so that's why he can't pick up."

"Out of town? Now? Where is he going?"

"Houston," I replied. "It's okay. We have a babysitter."

"You do? Who is it?"

"Bree. Remember her? Burton's cousin who's not a pirate or a vampire?" There was a long silence on the other end. "Mom? Mom, are you still there?"

Eventually, I heard noise, but I couldn't make out any clear words. I think I get my habit of muttering from Mom.

"Are you coming back soon?" I asked.

"We're working on something, but there's no guarantees," she said. "Are you three doing all right?"

"We're . . . fine," I said, deciding not to tell her about the attack on our decorations. "We're just, you know, worried."

"I know. Don't worry. We're okay here. Aunt Jane is spoiling us."

Pictures and recorded clips of my aunt spun up in my mind — her big smile, her loud laugh, the way she called people "dunderheads" when they deserved it. Suddenly, I was pining for her as much as I was pining for Mom and Lily. "Hey, Mom. Can I talk to Aunt Jane?"

"Sure. She's right here. Just a second."

I could hear a clunk and some murmurs and then my aunt's voice came on, saying, "Hey, you!"

"Hi, Aunt Jane. I miss you." For some reason, my voice went all squeaky and crackly.

"You all right, Dawnie?"

I was tempted to say no and start bawling, but I stopped myself just in time. What if I related all our miseries to Aunt Jane and she went and told Mom and Lily? They would just feel extra awful because they were stuck and couldn't help. Or what if she or Mom ended up telling Dad and he turned his car around and came home? He'd lose out on the deal he'd been working hard to get and he'd be stuck in a small, couchless apartment until the end of time, all because I'd been a crybaby.

I swallowed hard and cleared my throat. "I'm fine," I said. "It's just . . . Do you have any suggestions on what we can get Mom for Christmas? Everything we buy is all wrong."

Aunt Jane let out a low whistle. "She's a tough one, isn't she? When she was little she wanted to be a bareback rider and kept asking for a horse every Christmas."

"Kind of sounds like Darby," I said.

"It does, doesn't it?"

"I don't think we could get her a horse. Even if the three of us pooled our money."

Aunt Jane chuckled. "That's all right. I think she's given up her dream of being a bareback rider."

"It's just . . ." I stopped and sighed into the phone. "Her tastes are awfully particular. What do you usually get her — if you don't mind me asking?"

"Every year I'm stumped on what to get her, too. I figure, if I can't guess her tastes, at least I can give her permission to pamper herself. Your mom works hard, and she's not good at letting herself relax and take it easy. So I get her gift certificates to one of those Austin spas, or credit at an online store where she can buy herself some earrings or whatever she might need."

"Huh. That's a great idea," I said. "I wish I were older and wiser like the Wise Men — I mean, Wise People. Maybe then this whole present-buying thing wouldn't be so tricky."

"Picking out gifts has nothing to do with age or wisdom. I mean, really. What's a baby going to do with frankincense?"

I grinned. I'd never really thought about that. "Thanks, Aunt Jane. I . . . I miss you."

"I miss you, too, Dawnie B. I don't want you to worry about Miss Lily and your mom, okay? I'm taking good care of them."

"I know you are."

It was silent for a couple of seconds. But it was a good kind of silence, not an awkward one. The kind when you just pause to smile — or swallow a lump in your throat.

Aunt Jane might have heard me swallow, because she asked, "You sure everything is all right down there?"

I doubted my ability to lie a second time, so I told a half truth. "Well, you know how it is. A couple of lousy things have transpired — like this infernal snowstorm."

"Your mom told me about the pageant auditions. And your dad's sofa. Sorry about all that."

"Thanks." I held the phone away from me as I swallowed again. There's something mighty powerful about a sincere "I'm sorry" when you're low.

"Remember, Dawnie, in every bad situation there's something to be learned. And it makes you stronger. You don't think I got this tough by sitting around on pillows eating candy all day, do you?"

"But what if you're having one bad situation after another?"

"Well . . . maybe you'll learn a lot. Or maybe you'll learn one big thing. I don't know. But when you get through it, you'll be strong like King Kong. You'll be able to beat me in arm wrestling."

I laughed.

"I'm real sorry to hear about the bad stuff, Dawnie."

"I'm tough like you, Aunt Jane. I'll get through it." Strangely enough, just as I said that, I felt kind of hardy and rugged and better able to handle things.

After all, I was going to be a U.S. president, and U.S. presidents had to deal with bad stuff every day. There was no time to be a wimpy wuss.

I'd come up with my very first campaign slogan.

CHAPTER FIFTEEN

Supply Mission

Darby

It's kind of strange when people who aren't related to you stay at your house. Everything is different enough to make things seem weird. It's like when a picture is hanging a little crooked, and even though it's not upside down, that little bit of wonkiness makes it look all wrong.

Bree only brought one bag with her, but by the afternoon her stuff seemed to be everywhere. And she was usually stretched out over the whole sofa, so if we wanted to sit in the living room we had to use one of the two armchairs or squat on the floor by the coffee table.

And it's not just the sharing of space that bothers me about having houseguests who aren't related to us. It's knowing that they're getting an inside look at how our family works.

When we see people at school or church or out on the town, they get to find out about us, but only as much as we let them. If they stay in our home, though, they can't help but see lots of other things.

They see that the door to one of our kitchen cabinets is broken, but we haven't gotten it fixed yet.

They see what brand of peanut butter we buy. And shampoo. And gummy vitamins. (And they see that most items are store brand rather than the more expensive kind.)

They see Mom's reminder notes about chores, like: "Delaney — Trash! Love, Mom" and "Darby — Quincy stinks! Bath time? Love, Mom" and "Dawn — Pick up Continental army before vacuuming. Love, Mom."

I guess if we were worried enough about it, we could have done chores to spiff up the place, but we didn't. Instead, we tried buying Mom a gift card online, but those places always asked for credit cards and we didn't have one. We took a few votes on which of our lousy gifts was best for Mom, but each time everyone voted for the thing she bought. So for most of the morning, we just watched the big purple blob on the TV weather station.

Later on, we had lunch. Bree made us macaroni and cheese out of the box, but she cooked the noodles too long, so it was like cheesy oatmeal. It was edible, though.

"Glad you liked it," she said as I put my bowl in the already-full sink. "Because we might have to have it again for dinner. I don't see a lot of other options here."

It occurred to us that Mom had planned to be here by now, and that she'd probably held off buying food since we were supposed to be with Dad at his apartment. As much as we liked peanut butter sandwiches and macaroni and cheese, we decided we needed a bigger selection, so we volunteered to go downtown and get a few groceries with some of the money Dad left. Bree volunteered to stay home and rest. I don't know why she would need to rest, since she hadn't done anything except make lunch and text on her phone, but I was glad it would just be me and my sisters. I needed things to feel familiar for a while.

We headed down the road toward the center of town — first in our "baby duckling" formation and then in a group as the road widened and we got curbs and sidewalks. We thought about stopping in at the Neighbors' to tell them that the Santa-napper struck us and share our sorrows over cocoa, but their car wasn't there. I looked at the empty spot on the porch table where old St. Nick had stood and felt sad, squeeze-y thumps in my chest.

"If only we had been able to solve the case for them," I said. "Maybe then the whole town would have been safe and our decorations wouldn't have been messed with."

"I bet we can still figure it out," Dawn said. "Clearly, Lucas is our lead suspect. I don't trust that guy."

"No way! If it's anyone, it's Ms. Woolcott. Remember how her Santa collection gave us the heebie-jeebies?" Delaney said.

"You're crazy, Delaney," Dawn said. "Whoever took that Santa was quiet and sneaky. Ms. Woolcott is about as stealthy as a giraffe in high heels."

"I'm not crazy — you are! At least Ms. Woolcott has a motive," Delaney said. "If Lucas wants something, all he has to do is ask his parents."

Dawn and Delaney were glaring at each other and their voices were starting to get louder. I could tell this was about to turn into a big fuss. That meant I needed to do something to calm them down.

"You both have good points. And honestly, I think Mrs. Higginbotham's phone call with her friend almost sounded like a confession," I chimed in. "But the fact is, we don't have a lick of evidence. We can't do anything without solid clues, so let's not jump to conclusions."

Dawn and Delaney glowered for a few more seconds. Then Dawn let out a sigh and grumbled, "You're right. I hate it when you're right and I'm wrong, but you're right. About the evidence part, anyway."

"It's good you're levelheaded, Darby," Delaney said. "Exasperating, but good."

I was relieved they had backed down. As much as we wanted to solve the case, it was clear that our own feelings were getting in the way. Dawn was still sore at Lucas for getting to be a Wise Person. Delaney resented Ms. Woolcott for calling the cops on us those few times (because Delaney's powerful lungs were usually the reason why). And if I were totally honest with myself, I'd have to confess that I never liked Mrs. Higginbotham much. But holding a grudge against someone isn't a reason to accuse them of a crime.

"I just wish there was something we could do," Dawn said.

We stood there, leaning against the Neighbors' fence, thinking and brooding. I stared off into the distance, Delaney bounced, and Dawn tapped the side of her chin, but no one shouted "Aha!" or "I know!" or "Eureka!" After a while, we realized that if we stood and pondered all day, we'd have nothing but peanut butter to eat for dinner. So we resumed our mission to buy groceries.

We continued down the road until we turned onto Main Street, and there was Forever's. It was so nice to see something familiar and comforting. My heart felt like it was being raised inside me like a flag on a pole. Without even consulting with each other, the three of us skipped the rest of the way there.

Forever's is one of our favorite places on the planet. It's a combination grocery store, pharmacy, and lunch counter that opened when Eisenhower was president. Its real name is Ever's, but we like to call it Forever's since it's been around so long. We love the old-timey soda fountain and barstools and the big display case with all the pies, pecan tarts, and lunch specials.

It seemed right that we should treat ourselves to some pie after that long walk and do the grocery shopping afterward. Since we were low on money after buying three gifts for Mom, we decided that instead of having a piece of pie each, we should vote on and split one piece instead. I voted for the pear-cranberry one because it looked lonely and ignored. Only one piece of it was missing, whereas the apple was half-gone and the blue-berry only had two pieces left.

"You know . . . we could each have a pecan tart instead, and it won't cost us that much," Delaney suggested.

"They are less expensive," Dawn pointed out.

"And there are a lot of them," I noticed.

So we each ordered a pecan tart. They were fresh out of the oven — hot and gooey and sweet. The warmth spread through me and made me feel snug. It was like the magic of the Neighbors' porch in a tiny pie shell.

Funny how a bite of the right dessert can sometimes fix what a million encouraging words can't.

After we ate, we were ready to shop. We filled our basket with things that didn't seem too complicated to make. Spaghetti noodles and a jar of prepared sauce, a couple cans of chili, plus a big bear-shaped container of gummy bears (my idea), some hot cocoa mix (Delaney's), and a bag of jumbo marshmallows (Dawn's).

We also kept a lookout for other potential gifts for Mom. Delaney was showing me a fake chandelier that's also an air freshener when I noticed someone standing by the greeting card rack. He seemed familiar, even from the back. Floppy, sandy-colored hair . . . The way he raked his fingers through his bangs as he browsed the cards on display . . . *Alex!*

I pointed him out to Delaney, and she dropped the plastic chandelier and zipped right over to him, going, "Alex! Alex! Alex!" Dawn heard her and sped over from the candy aisle.

When he saw us, Alex's eyes grew as big and round as the pecan tarts. "Hi," he said. Only he said it kind of high and quick — like the yip of a small dog.

"Did you hear?" Delaney said. "There's a big purple blob over Boston!"

"Lily is stranded!" I said.

"She might not even make it back in time for Christmas!" Dawn said.

Alex nodded. "I know. I talked to her. I hope the weather clears. Apparently, there's a chance it might — a small chance."

"I hope so," I said.

"It just won't be Christmas without Lily," Delaney said.

"I know," Alex said, his voice low and mournful-sounding.

Dawn bunched up her face. "By the way, Alex, what happened the other day when we saw you downtown? You ran off like a puma was chasing you."

"Oh, that. I . . . um . . ." Alex shoved his hands in his jacket pockets and made twisty motions with his feet. "I just remembered something important. Sorry about that. Did you . . . um . . . did you tell Lily about seeing me?"

The three of us shook our heads.

"Why?" Dawn asked.

Alex smiled crookedly. "No reason. No big deal. There's really no point in mentioning it."

"Alex, are you all right?" I asked. "You seem . . . flustered."

"Discombobulated," Delaney said.

"Weird," Dawn said.

"Don't worry," Alex said. He still seemed jittery, but his eyes relaxed as he looked at us, making him appear enough like his old self. "I'm just a little stressed. That's all."

"You should come over and hang out with us," Delaney said. "We could play Presidential Trivia or Spite and Malice."

"Or we could Christmas shop. You could help us decide what to give Mom and we could help you with your gift for Lily," Dawn suggested.

"Right. I mean, no. I mean . . ." Alex's eyes looked skittish again, and his head turned every which way.

"Yeah, I gotta go. See you!" With a final dip of his head, he turned and stalked out of the store.

We watched through the window until he'd disappeared from view.

"What's up with Alex?" I asked.

"That's it," Dawn said, folding her arms across her chest. "I'm boycotting Christmas."

"Me, too," Delaney said. "What's up with this holiday? One by one everyone we love either gets taken away from us or goes looney tunes."

CHAPTER SIXTEEN

Proof Through the Night

Delaney

For dinner that night we had barbecue spaghetti. It was supposed to be regular spaghetti and meatballs, but Bree accidentally used barbecue sauce instead of the marinara sauce we bought. Also, the meatballs wouldn't hold together and she cooked the pasta too long again. So it was meat chunks and mush with a really zingy flavor. Dawn complained a little but ate most of hers. Darby was sad and pouty and hardly touched it. I actually liked it and ate all of mine and the rest of Darby's serving.

Before we sat down to eat, Dad called us on Mom's office phone to let us know he'd made it to Houston and that everything was set for the next day's surgery. We reassured him that all was good with us. We tried calling Mom and Lily but didn't get an answer, so we figured that they were on the phone with the airline.

It was sad and peculiar that everyone else in the family was out of town. Just a few days ago, Dawn, Darby, and I were worried about things like having enough decorations and getting cast as dumb angels. Now Bree was making us dinner and if we needed to talk with Dad, Mom, or Lily, we had to call them. I tried not to think about it, but occasionally I did and felt all woebegone.

It reminded me of those stories about poor kids growing up in London or some other big, grimy city. The children are always called "waifs" or "urchins," and they never have parents around, and all sorts of unfortunate things happen to them.

Okay, I guess that's a bit dramatic. Our parents were fine, they were just out of town. And no one had consumption or scurvy or any of those other awful-sounding old diseases. But we did have a no-good thug mess up our Christmas decorations, and we were probably going to have a lonely holiday.

Also, the food Bree cooked was kind of like gruel. I don't exactly know what gruel is, but I know it's mushy. And it was starting to look as if we lived in squalor. The house — especially the kitchen — was filling up with mess, and no one was cleaning.

I was just about to suggest that we scrub our dishes when the doorbell rang. Then it rang again. And again. And a fourth time.

"Who's the nuisance?" Bree asked. "Are you expecting anyone?"

The three of us shook our heads. The doorbell rang twice more, so Darby walked up and asked loudly, "Who is it?"

"It's Josie Woolcott, from next door," came a muffled voice. "Please open up! Something awful has happened!"

Darby opened the door and Ms. Woolcott rushed right on in, saying, "It's horrible! Ab-so-LUTE-ly horrible! I've been invaded! My house has been attacked!"

We'd never seen her so twitchy and distressed-looking, and for a moment, all we could do was gape at her. Adding to the confusion, we could hear a thin, high-pitched version of "Deck the Halls." It took me a while to realize it was coming from her sweater. This one had gingerbread men dancing and holding hands with big grins on their faces. A twisty green garland above them flashed tiny lights while the music played.

We cleared some of Bree's stuff off a sofa cushion and

had her sit between Dawn and Darby. I stood behind her and fanned her with a copy of *Texas Monthly*. Meanwhile, Bree sat in one of the armchairs and watched it all unfold.

Eventually, the tinny sweater music stopped, Ms. Woolcott finished bemoaning the fact that evil knaves would target a defenseless lady, and everything grew quiet — except for the *flip-flip* sounds of me fanning her with the magazine. Even though Ms. Woolcott had calmed down, I was still really focused on it and wanted to see if I could get her hair to move.

"Can you tell us what happened?" Dawn asked.

Ms. Woolcott took a deep breath and blinked several times. "I had just finished baking my king cake for the ladies' club holiday potluck, and I set it outside to cool off before I took it out of the pan," she began shakily. "I put it on the bench on my porch and then went back inside to feed Elvis. When I was done, I stepped out to get the cake, and it was gone! Com-PLETE-ly gone!"

"Did you see or hear anything?" Darby asked.

Ms. Woolcott shook her head. "No. I wasn't near the window. And I always sing to Elvis when I feed and brush him, so I didn't hear a thing."

I stopped fanning. "What do you sing to him?" I asked.

Dawn and Darby gave me confused looks.

"Beg your pardon?" Ms. Woolcott asked, turning slightly so she could see me.

"I said . . . um . . . was anything else stolen?"

"No, not that I saw," Ms. Woolcott said. "I just can't believe someone would do this. Especially at Christmas! Especially to a helpless person like me!"

On the word *me*, Ms. Woolcott whacked the top of her chest, and suddenly her sweater started flashing and playing "Deck the Halls" again.

"Who would do such a thing?" she wailed over the *fa-la-las*. "I've never hurt anyone!"

It was true. Ms. Woolcott was a busybody, but she never harmed a soul as far as I know — at least, not on purpose. It was true villainy that someone would abscond with her cake.

Finally, Ms. Woolcott slumped back onto the couch. "My stars, I haven't been this upset in a while. You all are so good to take me in during this crisis. Especially when you have so much to take care of yourselves." She sat forward and glanced around our messy living room. Eventually, her eyes landed on Bree. "Oh! Who is this?"

"That's Bree, our babysitter," I explained. "She was a bridesmaid at the Almost Wedding last summer. Remember? Bree, this is our neighbor Ms. Woolcott."

"Charmed," Bree said, sounding kind of British.

"How do you do?" Ms. Woolcott said back.

The last *la-las* died out and everything got quiet again. Ms. Woolcott seemed a little stiff and nervous now that she'd realized Bree was there. She smiled awkwardly and kept smoothing her hair as if it were messy. But it wasn't. Even after all my fanning.

"Maybe we can help you catch the cake thief," Darby said to Ms. Woolcott.

"That's sweet, dear, but what on earth could you do?"

"We could look for clues," I suggested.

"Yes, just like we did at the Neighbors' property," Darby said.

"You don't mean . . ." Ms. Woolcott pressed her hand to her chest. This time the sweater stayed quiet. "Do you think this was the work of the same thief who took the Neighbors' candy Santa?"

"Yep," I said. "And the same scoundrel who wrecked our Christmas decorations."

"Ms. Woolcott, we want to apprehend this evildoer as much as you do," Dawn said. "Would it be all right if we searched your porch for evidence?"

"Well . . . I don't see why not," she replied. "It's dark out, but my porch light is bright enough for you to see. Just make sure your dog stays here. I don't want to upset poor Elvis."

We agreed, and Bree said for us to not go anyplace else and to come back after half an hour. We agreed to that, too. Then we followed Ms. Woolcott back to her house, making sure Quincy stayed behind.

As we mounted her porch steps, Ms. Woolcott said in a shaky voice, "Here we are. The scene of the crime."

We promised we'd let her know if we found anything, and she went on into the house. We could hear her comforting Elvis, as if he were the one who was upset instead of her. Elvis, of course, just said, "*Myrrh.*"

For twenty minutes we scoured the porch as best we could in the yellow, bug-infested light of Ms. Woolcott's porch, but we found nothing — just an empty striped snail shell that Darby wanted to keep for herself.

"I don't know," Darby said as she finished examining Ms. Woolcott's flowerpots. "Are we sure this is the same miscreant who messed up our porch and stole St. Nick? Maybe it was someone else. Maybe all three acts were done by different people. Maybe our town is full of hooligans." She sounded sad. I didn't blame her. It was bad enough to think of one rogue on the loose. But a whole slew of them?

Dawn sat down on the top step of the porch and said, "Come on, gang. Let's review the facts."

Darby and I sat on either side of her.

"So what do we know about these events?" she asked. "What do they have in common?"

"Well . . . all three offenses were committed on the same street," Darby said.

"Right," Dawn said. "So what could that mean?"

"He hates our street!" I said.

"Or," Darby said, "he or she lives in this area. Or comes this way regularly."

"Right. And all three happened on porches," Dawn said. "So what could that mean?"

"He hates porches!" I said.

"It might mean that he's not a major thief," Darby said. "He or she doesn't break into homes or cars. Everything he's done or taken — they're minor infractions. But it still stinks."

"And it always happens at night," Dawn pointed out. "So that could mean that he knows what he's doing is wrong. He has to do it under cover of darkness."

"Like a ninja," I said.

"Or a low-life sneak," Dawn said.

"This is helpful," Darby said. "What else do the incidents have in common?"

"Well, let's see . . ." Dawn tapped her chin. "He took a Santa and a king cake and he tore down our decorations . . ."

"He hates Christmas!" I said.

"Maybe," Dawn said, still tapping her chin. "He could be a Grinch type or a Scrooge."

"I bet he has an evil laugh, too," I said. "It probably goes something like, 'HEH heh heh heh!' or 'Mwa ha ha ha!'"

"Delaney, that's just a hunch," Dawn said. "I'm talking about something based on information and evidence."

I knew what she meant, but I couldn't help it. I already had in my mind an image of a little bitty man with a cackling laugh who sneaks around all hunched over and spoils people's Christmas cheer. Maybe he hated Christmas for a reason. Maybe he never received the presents he asked for. Or maybe his parents were always gone at Christmastime. Or maybe he never got the part he wanted in the Christmas Eve Pageant and it warped his brain.

"The thing is, we don't have any real evidence," Darby said. "We don't have physical clues or eyewitnesses or —"

"I got it!" I leaped to my feet, ran down the rest of the steps, and started bouncing around in front of the porch. I was so happy with my thought, I almost forgot to share it with them.

Finally, Dawn shouted, "What, Delaney? What's your plan?"

"We need to do a Neighborhood Watch."

CHAPTER SEVENTEEN

Diplomacy

Dawn

Hold up," Bree said, meeting us at the bottom of the stairs.

We'd just finished gathering all the materials we would need for the Neighborhood Watch. We had our walkie-talkies and flashlights and a couple of bungee cords and a pair of toy handcuffs we found in the closet. Plus, Darby was carrying a badminton racquet. We were headed to the kitchen to pack up some gummy bears and peanut butter sandwiches, so that we could keep up our strength on the mission.

"Where do you guys think you're going?" Bree asked.

"The kitchen," Delaney said.

Bree looked annoyed. "I mean after that."

"We're doing a Neighborhood Watch to keep our street safe from that low-life Christmas thief," Darby said.

"Nope. You aren't," Bree said in a flat voice. She says everything in a flat voice, so at first I thought she was joking.

"Ha-ha. Very funny," I said. "There's just a couple more provisions we need and then we'll be out of your hair."

"I mean it, guys. I can't let you go out there on your own in the dark. Especially" — she reached over and plucked the racquet out of Darby's hands — "with any sort of weaponry."

"But why?" we said a whiny chorus.

"Look . . ." Bree blew out her breath and started chipping at her black nail polish. "I know I act all laissez-faire, but I really do take this job seriously. I need to be responsible and keep you safe, and that means there's no way I can let you run around outside after dark."

"But we need to save the neighborhood!" Delaney wailed. "We're doing a good thing. We're keeping an eye out for that little Grinchy guy and making sure he doesn't ruin anyone else's holiday!"

"First of all, Neighborhood Watch does not mean vigilante justice," Bree said, pointing to the handcuffs that were hanging off Delaney's belt loop. "Secondly, if there is a criminal afoot, a patrol of eleven-year-olds is not the answer."

"But the cops can't do anything, so we have to!" I said.

"It's our civic duty!" Darby said.

"We can't just stand by and do nothing!" Delaney said.

"Sorry, gang. You can watch from the windows. That's the best I can offer."

I could tell that whining and arguing and stamping our feet weren't going to get us anywhere with Bree. She was sort of like Mom that way.

"The thing is," I began, trying to make my voice calm and grown-up sounding, "it's very dark outside. So if we watch out the windows, all we will see is dark. It would be a hopeless Neighborhood Watch if all we did is stare into a black void, don't you agree?"

Bree tilted her head and looked at me. Her eyes narrowed so that all I could see was eyeliner. "Well played," she said with a tiny smile. "But it's still a no-go. Sorry."

The three of us moaned "Aww!" at the same time.

"Hey, just doing my job," she said with a shrug. "If I could invent some way for you to see in the dark, I would."

Something she said made my mind go backward, like flipping pages in reverse to find something you'd read earlier in a book. Eventually, a picture sprang up in my brain of someone in the dark, with green glowing spectacles . . .

"Lucas!" I shouted.

I raced into Mom's office and pulled out our church directory. The Westbrook home number was listed on the last page. By the time I'd finished punching in the digits, Darby, Delaney, and Bree had caught up with me and were standing inside the doorway, watching. Darby looked worried, Delaney looked confused, and Bree looked intrigued.

After a couple of rings, someone picked up and said, "Westbrook residence. Lucas speaking."

"Lucas, it's Dawn Brewster."

"Hi, Dawn. Guess what! I got a hat that was signed by a baseball player! I don't know who it is and I can't read his writing, but he's a real professional player and everything."

"That's great, Lucas. Hey, listen. We need your help."

"You do?"

"Yes. We're keeping a watch for the Santa-napper and we need to borrow your night vision goggles." I figured Lucas wouldn't just lend his presents willy-nilly, so I decided to make a strong case for his assistance. "It's real important, Lucas. It's a matter of public safety. It's a matter of justice and the American way. It's a matter of life, liberty, and the pursuit of happiness!"

"Okay. But I'll have to ask my mom." I could hear him set down the phone, and then there was a muffled conversation in the background.

"What's going on?" Delaney asked, bouncing on the toes of her sneakers.

"*Shhhh!*" I said.

I could hear a clunk and rattle as someone picked up the phone, and then Lucas said, "She says it's all right. But she also says you'll need to come get it because she's making fruitcake for the Christmas Eve Pageant."

I felt a little thud behind my ribs. If Mom were here, she'd be making those sugar cookies. And maybe a cobbler or two.

"I'd take it over there on my bike," Lucas went on, "but I'm not allowed to leave by myself after dark."

"I understand that. We're bound by the same rule," I said. "Hang on a sec, Lucas. Let me ask our babysitter." I put the phone up against my leg to cover the speaker part. "Bree, we agree to abide by your rules and watch from the windows. But do you think you could drive us

down the street to pick up an important piece of sur-
veillance gear?"

Bree made another one of her kinda-sorta smiles that
look a little like a smirk. "Sure thing," she said.

"We're on our way, Lucas!" I shouted into the phone.
Then I hung up and raced for the door.

It seemed to take forever for everyone to get their
coats on and pile into Bree's little red car. Bree followed
my directions, and soon we were pulling up in front of
the Westbrook house.

"I always wondered who lived in this big place,"
Bree said.

"Lucas does. With his parents," Delaney said.

"Really?" Bree made a whistling sound. "That's a lot
of house for only three people."

"Yeah, you don't want to play hide-and-seek there,"
Darby said. "Especially if you're sleepy."

They stayed in the car while I hopped out and ran up
the walkway to the door. Lucas opened it a split second
after I rang the bell. He must have been standing right
on the other side.

"Here you go," he said, handing me the goggles. "I
also brought down some other things I thought might
help. Could you use a telescope?"

"I don't think so. Not unless it's also night vision."

"Oh. Right." He bent over and picked up a couple of other items. "What about a lasso or a casting net?"

My mouth fell open. "You know how to lasso?"

Lucas looked kind of embarrassed. "Well . . . not yet. I'm taking lessons. Can you?"

"No, but we want to. Maybe you could give us some pointers?"

"Sure!" Lucas smiled so big, his braces gleamed under the big chandelier light in the foyer.

"Well, thanks for the loan," I said, holding up the goggles. "We'll be real careful with them." I spun around and started trotting down the sidewalk toward Bree's car.

"Wait!" Lucas came out after me. "If you can't lasso yet, that won't help you. But go ahead and take the net, just in case."

He pressed the net into my hands and our fingers touched. That was kind of awkward, especially since it took a while for him to untangle his hands. Still, it was thoughtful of him.

Why was he being so nice to us, anyway? Was it just to annoy me? Was it a trick?

I stood there, feeling confused, as I watched him walk back into his house. Maybe Lucas was more than just a spoiled show-off. I wasn't exactly sure if he was a good guy, but I felt certain — somehow — that he wasn't a bad guy.

"Stage one complete," I said as I climbed in the backseat next to my sisters.

The others were impressed by the night vision goggles and the big net.

"Wow! That boy has everything," Darby said. I could tell by the fired-up look in her eye that she was already concocting crazy schemes involving that net.

"Don't even think about trying out new stunts, Darby," Bree said. In the rearview mirror, I could see her cock an eyebrow.

Bree was another surprise today. She was turning out to be a decent babysitter, which I suppose was good news overall, but it was also kind of discouraging for our plans.

Darby hung her head. "It never occurred to me," she lied.

Delaney leaned across Darby and said, "So, Dawn. Since you told Lucas about our Neighborhood Watch, does this mean you don't think he's a suspect anymore?"

I shrugged. I wasn't exactly sure why I felt better about Lucas, only that I did. "I figure the only way we can catch this culprit is if we all band together as friends and neighbors, so I've decided to trust him."

Darby and Delaney gave me strange looks.

"You?" Darby asked.

"Hey, you're always saying I should have faith in the good of people instead of the bad," I reminded her. "So I'm trying it."

Darby smiled. "Good."

"But," I added, "I'm not making any promises."

CHAPTER EIGHTEEN

The Common Defense

Darby

Neighborhood Watch is boring," Delaney said. She was bouncing on her bed, wearing six different hats. It made her outline look strange in the faint light.

We realized that in order to really scan the darkness outside with the goggles, we had to make it dark inside, too. So we turned out all the lights inside and outside the house. We also figured out that the window in the Triangular Office had the best view of our front yard and a side view of Ms. Woolcott's house.

That's why we were all upstairs. In the dark. And bored.

Well . . . Dawn wasn't. She'd been sitting at the window for an hour already and was showing no signs of giving up.

At first we'd taken turns with the goggles, but Delaney couldn't sit still with them for even five minutes. And when I wore them, Dawn kept fussing at me for looking up at the sky. "Ding-dang it, Darby! Do you think the Santa-napper's going to parachute out of a stealth airplane?" But I couldn't help it. At first it was cool seeing everything in night vision, but after a while, you realized you were just looking at an empty yard, only with a greenish glow. The stars, at least, were interesting.

Finally, it was Dawn's turn, and it just sort of stayed her turn.

Even Quincy had gotten bored. He'd been wandering around, whimpering and sighing, until we finally asked if he wanted to go in his crate. Poor dog practically dug through the front door to get to where we'd set his kennel on the porch. At least it wasn't that cold. And we figured he could warn us if anyone got close to our house. Still, when a playful Labrador prefers sleeping in a cage to hanging out with you, you know you're at a pretty excruciating level of boring.

While Dawn watched and Delaney bounced, Bree and I sat on the floor and played Go Fish using the weak beam of a flashlight with nearly used-up batteries. She wasn't all that into it, though. I could tell because she barely looked at her cards and kept making mistakes.

"You know what we should do, as long as it's dark like this?" Bree said. "We should hold a séance."

"What's a séance?" Delaney asked.

"It's when you communicate with the souls of the departed," Bree said.

"You mean dead people?" I asked.

"That's a load of hogwash," Dawn said.

"Why would anyone do such a thing?" Delaney asked.

"To ask questions, and find out stuff," Bree said. "Sometimes people learn family secrets or messages from loved ones — or even where money or treasure is hidden."

"I'll do it!" I said. "I would love to talk to a spirit!"

"What about you, Delaney?" Bree asked.

"Maybe. Who would we talk to?"

"I know!" I said, raising my hand. "We could communicate with the bathroom ghost!"

We're pretty sure our mom's bathroom is haunted. For as long as we can remember we've heard strange noises in that room — knocks and moans and occasionally a bellow. If we could talk to him, we could ask him why he keeps hanging around. And why the bathroom? Why not, say, the coat closet or the pantry?

"No! I don't want to talk to the bathroom ghost," Delaney said.

"I don't, either," Dawn said. "And I still say it's a bunch of hooey."

Dawn and Delaney are scared of the ghost. I don't know why. If he could hurt us he would have already tied us up with toilet paper or something.

"Okay, then," Bree said. She stood up and smoothed out her skirt and stockings. "If you could have a conversation with anyone who used to be alive, who would you want to talk to?"

I was just thinking it was a tough question when Dawn said, "That's easy. George Washington."

"Really?" Bree said. She sounded a little disappointed. "Well, all right, let's contact George Washington."

"Yay! He'll be nice to talk to," Delaney said, bouncing even higher on her bed and making the stack of hats fall off her head.

"So how do we contact him?" I asked.

"Well, you sit in a circle around a candle, and if you have any objects of the deceased, you put those in the center," Bree explained.

"Um, Bree?" Delaney was leaning forward and tugging on Bree's sweater. "Since we never met him when he was alive — you know, because he lived two hundred years ago — we actually don't have anything of his."

"I know! What about the George Globes?" I suggested.

First we had to explain to Bree what those were, and then she said they should be perfect. "Anything imbued with his essence or likeness. Or things that were important to him in life," Bree explained. "Hey! You guys have a flag, right?"

We did have a flag — properly folded and stored downstairs. Only there is strict etiquette regarding the display and use of the American flag. Nothing in the rules mentions conjuring the ghosts of departed presidents, so we held a mini meeting to decide. Since it wouldn't be flying on a pole, would be placed near fire, and would be utilized for a personal and supernatural purpose rather than a dignified display of patriotism, we unanimously voted not to use it.

"And anyway, he wouldn't recognize it, since the flag only had fifteen stars on it by the time he died," I said.

"And anyway, this whole thing is malarkey," Dawn said, still facing forward and staring out the window.

Delaney and I took the flashlight and headed downstairs to gather what we needed. There was a George Globe in the ornament box that we couldn't rehang, because the hook cracked off when the Santa-napper struck our house, so we grabbed it. We also got a couple of dollar bills that weren't cut up, a few quarters, postage stamps with flags on them, the candlestick and candle from the fireplace mantel, a book of matches, some gummy bears and marshmallows to snack on, and an old tin tray painted with apples, pears, cherries, and pineapples — because we needed something safe and sturdy to put the candle on, and also because Washington grew fruit trees on his land (although probably not pineapples).

It was kind of spooky walking around the house in the dark — especially without Mom or Dad or Lily there. All our furniture looked colorless and mournful, as if it felt sad and lonely without anyone around to use it. And the rushes of wind outside sounded like the breath of a giant napping beast.

I like spooky because it makes me feel extra alive. But Delaney doesn't, so she kept whirling around and saying, "Did you hear something?" and would zoom really fast by Mom's bathroom. At one point she caught sight of her reflection in the small mirror by the door and made a noise like "*Yipe!*"

When we got back upstairs, we saw that Bree had cleared out a spot on our messy floor and Dawn was still on watch. We put our findings on the rug and carefully set the candle on the tin tray. Then Bree, Delaney, and I sat cross-legged around the items.

"Dawn? Aren't you going to join us?" Delaney asked.

Dawn made a huffy sound. "I'm helping to maintain the security of our neighborhood. I don't have time to hobnob with apparitions."

"But it was your idea," I pointed out.

"Yeah," Delaney said. "He's your favorite president. He's why you made the George Globes, and you always say you want to model your own presidency after his."

"If he's your favorite and you already feel a strong connection to him, you should join the circle," Bree said. "Your presence would be powerful, and it's more likely to work with you."

Even with the darkness and the weird contraption on her head, I could see Dawn perk up a bit. She always did enjoy feeling powerful. She raised her head and tapped her finger against her chin.

"As much as I'd like to help you guys, I am on an important assignment here," she said.

"It's just for a little while. Just until we make contact," Bree said. "There's no way a thief will be able to sneak around and do damage in just a few minutes, right?"

Dawn cocked her head and tapped her jaw again. She seemed to be considering it.

"All right, fine," she said. "But only because you guys seem kind of aimless without me. I reserve the right to quit whenever I've had my fill of this." She stood up, set the goggles on the chair, and sat down on the rug between me and Bree.

Bree took the box of matches and lit the candle on the tin tray. I turned off the flashlight.

"Now what?" Delaney asked.

"Now we hold hands, close our eyes, and call out with our minds."

I wasn't sure how to call out with my mind, but I did grab hold of Delaney's and Dawn's hands.

"Oh, Mr. Washington —" Bree began.

"Ahem," Dawn interrupted. "You really should address him as Mr. President."

"Fine," Bree said in her regular voice. Then she shut her eyes and said, "Oh, Mr. President Washington . . . we, your followers and descendants, ask you to sit and, you know, hang out with us for a while, talk about old times . . ."

For some reason, Delaney started humming a slowed-down version of "Yankee Doodle." I joined in, and after a couple of lines so did Dawn. Meanwhile, Bree kept talking.

"Come to us . . . Let us know what you think about our country today . . . its fashions . . . and, um . . ." Bree leaned sideways toward Dawn and whispered, "Anything you want to add?"

"Tell us if we are on the right path as a nation," Dawn said loudly. Meanwhile, Delaney and I kept humming. "Tell us if we've lost our way . . . Tell us about your favorite and least favorite amendments . . . Tell us what you think of the electoral college . . ."

For someone who thought it was a bunch of nonsense, Dawn was really getting into it.

"Oh, Mr. President," Dawn went on, the lower part of her face lit up by the candle, "if you are here with us now, give us a sign!"

"*Wowoooooooh!*"

"*Aaaaaaaaaaah!*" shouted the four of us at once. I guess the sudden gust of breath from all directions was too much for the candle. The flame went out instantly.

There was a lot of bustling, and I couldn't tell what was happening. I reached out and rummaged around for the flashlight, but instead grabbed the George

Globe and someone's foot. The owner of the foot screeched and hopped away from me.

"There's a person outside the house!" yelled someone.

I could see the outline of Dawn at the window, the night vision goggles back on her head.

"Is it George Washington?" I asked.

"Is it a little hunched-over cackling man?" Delaney asked.

"I can't tell who it is," Dawn said. "It certainly doesn't look like George Washington or a hunched-over man, but it is a man."

"I bet it's the Santa-napper!" Delaney said. "He's come back!"

"I bet he thinks no one is home because all the lights are out," Bree said.

"Let me see." I held my hands toward Dawn, and she took off the night vision goggles and handed them to me. I put them on and stared out at the lawn. Sure enough, the glowing figure of a tall person was down there pacing up and down in the yard, looking at our house.

An icy sensation spread through me, like when I drink a slushy too fast — only worse.

Quincy was barking like crazy, and I suddenly realized that the howl we'd heard had come from him, not a ghost. Dawn must have figured that out before me and checked the window.

As I watched, I saw the glowing person head toward the house. Soon I couldn't even see him anymore. In between Quincy's barks, I could hear footsteps.

"He's on our porch!" I said.

"We should call the cops!" Dawn shouted.

"But the phone is downstairs, where the Grinchy guy is," Delaney said in a whimpery voice.

"Bree, use your cell," I said.

"I can't." Bree sounded really upset. "It's downstairs charging."

I turned from the window and looked at their glowing, worried faces. "So what do we do?"

CHAPTER NINETEEN

Runoff

Delaney

You know when people talk about being in a stressful situation and they describe how their heart beats really fast, but everything around them goes in slow motion? Well, it really can happen like that.

After we realized we were trapped upstairs with the Santa-napper on our porch, we came up with a plan — a good one. But I was still scared.

All that extra energy was building up inside me, like it usually does when I'm feeling a strong feeling. Only I couldn't run around or turn cartwheels, and I thought I was going to explode right there in the Triangular Office. I wondered if it would make a loud noise when I burst apart, and if I'd end up in pieces or a pile of goo.

And then I realized that I would never know — because I'd be too exploded to comprehend it — and that made me extra bummed.

"Keep still, Delaney," Darby whispered to me as we gathered at the top of the stairs.

I was wiggling and making noises like a sad puppy. Not on purpose. The squirmy energy was just sneaking out in places.

"Okay, does everyone know their part?" Dawn whispered.

Darby, Bree, and I all said yes in real quiet voices.

"You sure?" Dawn asked. "Speak now if you're confused or feel like you're too yellow-bellied to go through with it."

No one said anything. I worked really hard to control the puppy sounds.

"All righty, then. Follow me."

Dawn led us down the stairs, all of us tiptoeing. She was wearing the goggles, so she was the only one who could see really well.

My heart was beating like a drum roll, and I was sure everyone else could hear it. I expected Dawn or Darby to tell me to shush at any moment.

We made it down the steps and crept down the

hall. Bree veered into Mom's office to call the police department, and the rest of us stepped quietly into the living room.

It was super spooky downstairs. It had seemed eerie before, when I'd come down with Darby, but knowing the Grinchy guy was outside made it extra ominous.

Dawn pointed toward the front windows, and the drum in my chest got faster. Through the thin curtains I could see someone walking around on our porch. Because it was dark, I could only make out his shape. He wasn't hunched over, but he was moving kind of sneakily. And he might have been cackling — it was hard to tell with Quincy barking so much.

We huddled by the door, and Dawn held up one finger, then two, then three, and . . .

Dawn yanked the door open and hollered "Now!" — and that's when everything started going in slow motion.

It was like a dance — a beautiful, slow dance with everyone doing their part perfectly. As soon as Dawn gave us our cue, I took a deep breath and let out one of my intolerably loud screams. I could see Darby charge forward, shooting the Grinchy guy with her marshmallow shooter. Even in the dark I could see the gleam of concentration on her face as she ran past me. I followed her, still screaming, and together we confused and startled the intruder. He held up his hands to avoid getting pelted (or maybe to plug his ears), and then Dawn rushed out and tossed the net over him.

It actually didn't go completely over him, as we'd hoped, but it did cover his upraised arms and get his hands all tangled.

The man exclaimed, "Hey!"

Dawn said, "Wait!"

I yelled, "We got you, Grinchy guy!"

The man said, "Is this another reenactment?"

Then, just when Darby was about to start restraining him with bungee cords, Dawn held out her arm to stop her.

"It's Alex!" Dawn shouted.

That's when everything whirred up to regular speed.

"Alex?" I said, looking over at the dark figure struggling to free his hands from the net.

Just then, the porch light went on and Bree came out. "Are you guys all right? . . . Oh!"

My eyes blinked to get used to the light, and then I could see it really was Alex. He freed his fingers, tossed down the net, and squinted at us. "What the . . . ?" he said. He gestured to the mess of netting and marshmallows all over the porch. "What's going on?"

"We thought you were the Grinchy guy," I said.

"The who?" he asked.

"The Santa-napper," Darby said.

"The no-good Scrooge person who's been terrorizing the neighborhood," Dawn explained.

"What are you doing here?" Bree asked him.

"Mr. Brewster asked me to check on you guys and make sure everything was going all right. But when I got here, it looked like no one was home. I thought that was kind of odd considering the time, and with the car here." He pointed to Bree's red hatchback.

"We were upstairs trying to talk to George Washington," I said. I had to shout because Quincy kept barking and barking.

"Quincy, it's okay," Darby said. "It's just Alex."

"Let him out so he can see," Dawn said.

I walked over to Quincy's crate and undid the latch. "See, Quincy. It's just our pal —"

Quincy pushed through the door and ran out. I expected him to race up to Alex and do one of his tail-wagging, slobbery greetings, but instead he took off like a streak across the yard and headed straight for the Neighbors' house.

"What's wrong with Quincy?" Bree asked.

"It's like he's after something," Alex said.

"The Santa-napper!" Dawn, Darby, and I said together. We raced off the porch and after our dog.

I could hear Bree yell something to us, but I couldn't tell what. I was too focused on catching up with Quincy.

We ran to the street, checked for traffic, and then crossed over to the Neighbors' property. We found Quincy standing right outside the garden shed, barking his fool head off and jumping up against the door and walls. I could tell by the growly way he was barking that he was upset. Whatever was in the shed, he saw it as a threat.

"I've never seen Quincy this worked up before," I said.

"I think the Santa-napper is in there," Darby said.

"Aw, man!" Dawn grumbled. "Why didn't we bring the net?"

Alex and Bree came up just then.

"You didn't happen to bring the net or the marshmallow shooter, did you?" Dawn asked.

"No," Alex said.

"What's all this commotion about?" called out someone behind us.

I turned around and saw Mr. Neighbor coming out of his house. He was wearing a coat over his robe and pajamas and carrying a flashlight.

"Quincy thinks the Santa-napper is in your shed," I explained.

Mr. Neighbor shook his head. "I don't see how. It's locked, and I'm the only one with the key." He reached in his coat pocket and pulled out a bunch of keys on a ring, holding them up so we could see.

"Maybe he got in some other way," Dawn said.

"He really does seem agitated," Alex said. "Maybe you should check?"

"Couldn't hurt," Mr. Neighbor said with a shrug.

"You girls should probably restrain your dog," Bree said. "Here. I brought the leash."

It took the three of us to hold on to Quincy and get his leash on him. Then, to be sure he didn't break away from us while Mr. Neighbor opened the shed, I held on to the leash handle while Dawn kept a hand on the back of his collar and Darby put her arms around his middle.

Mr. Neighbor took his key, undid the lock, and slowly pulled open the door.

I was bouncing so nervously, I was jumping up and down. But I held tight to the leash. Quincy kept on barking and straining to get away.

At first, all we could see was darkness inside the shed. I started to think we'd made a big mistake, but then

something went *clank!* and I could see faint movement —
like a twisting of the shadows.

"There really is something in there," Alex said.

I shouted, "Watch out!" and waited for a hunched-
over man to scurry out of there, cackling his evil cackle.

"You should all stand back," Mr. Neighbor said. He
stepped forward and pointed the flashlight beam into
the shed.

I held my breath as the light bounced off the walls,
but I didn't see anything. Then we heard another
clank! Mr. Neighbor tilted the light down toward the
noise . . .

And there was the small hunched-over man! He had
glowing yellow eyes and was wearing a mask!

I couldn't help it. I let out one of my intolerable
screams, and the little man went racing past me into
the yard. Mr. Neighbor kept the flashlight on him the
whole way.

And that's when I noticed the fur. And the pointy
nose, and the striped tail.

The hunched-over Grinchy guy was a big raccoon.

"Well, what do you know?" Mr. Neighbor said. "I did
have an intruder."

The raccoon looked at us for a second and then took
off into the darkness. Quincy wanted to run after it real

bad, but we held on to him tight and told him it was okay in a calm voice. Eventually, he settled down a bit and his barking turned to whines.

Mr. Neighbor pulled a string hanging down from the shed's ceiling and a light came on inside. We found a rusty section where a piece of the wall was missing and realized that's what the raccoon had used as a door.

"And lookee here," Mr. Neighbor said. He was standing in a back corner, by a stack of flowerpots.

He moved aside a tarp so that we could get closer and there, in a pile, was a collection of Christmas things. There were half-eaten candy canes from our porch, bits of tinsel, Ms. Woolcott's cake pan, a chewed-up miniature pumpkin, and Mr. Neighbor's priceless Santa figurine. The top half of St. Nick was on one part of the pile and the bottom half was way on the other side. All of the candy was missing, and only a few ripped-up wrappers remained.

"The Santa-napper was a raccoon?" Dawn said.

"Looks like it," Alex said.

At this point, Mrs. Neighbor had come out on the back stoop in her coat and slippers. Bree went over to fill her in on what had happened.

Meanwhile, Dawn and I continued to keep hold of Quincy, but Darby let go to help Mr. Neighbor. She picked up the lower half of the figurine and handed it to him, asking, "Is St. Nick going to be okay?"

Mr. Neighbor brushed some dirt and grass off the figure and gently put him back together. "He's a little grimy, but he's back. I'm mighty glad to see him. I thank you girls for the gift."

"But we didn't give him to you," I pointed out. "You already had him."

"I'm not talking about St. Nick," Mr. Neighbor said. "I'm talking about you helping to find him. You never gave up, and now he's back home. Helping people out is a gift. In fact, it's what Christmas is all about."

As Mr. Neighbor gently carried his Santa figure out of the shed, blinking lights seemed to bounce off the two of them, illuminating them in a reddish glow. It looked like a real Christmas miracle was happening right before our eyes.

And then I saw the police cars parked on the street.

CHAPTER TWENTY

Profile in Courage

Dawn

There were two whole cop cars with their lights flashing, and four police officers! Bree had called them about our intruder and then called them back when she realized it was Alex. But Ms. Woolcott had heard my intolerable screaming and she called them, too, so they figured something terrible was happening and raced over!" Delaney was talking faster than her feet could bounce.

"Whoa," Lucas said. He let his mouth hang open, and his eyes were all shiny.

"Then Mr. Neighbor explained about the raccoon," Delaney went on. "And I told them that Santa had been kidnapped, but that we found him in the shed."

"That's so cool," Lucas said.

"I know," Delaney said. "Bree said this has been the most splendid job she's ever had. She said she'll be sad when Dad gets home this evening and that her house will be boring after everything that happened last night."

"Yeah, I wish I'd been there to see all that," Lucas grumbled, staring down at the floor. Or maybe he was looking at his new remote-controlled T. rex. It was hard to tell.

"You helped a lot," I said. "Thanks for letting us borrow your net and goggles. That's why we came over, really. We wanted to return your things."

"Oh," he said, still sounding glum. "You guys can keep them longer if you want."

"Really?" Darby said. "Can we keep the net for a few weeks?"

I shook my head at her. "Forget it, Darby. Don't even think about doing stunts."

"Fine," Darby said in a sad voice. "Thanks for loaning us these, Lucas," she said, handing over the night vision goggles. "We couldn't have cracked the case without your help."

"Really?" Lucas said, setting them on the air hockey table behind him.

"Really," I said.

I stepped forward and handed him the casting net. Apparently, my fingers got a little jumbled up in it while I was standing there, waiting for Delaney to tell the whole story, so it took a little while to untangle myself. And when Lucas grabbed it from me, his fingers came right through the holes and touched mine. I felt kind of squeamish, and I couldn't stop thinking about how close he was standing to me, so I fumbled a lot more than usual. Finally, I got free.

"You are really brave," Lucas said. "I can't believe you threw the net over a real live prowler."

A hot, stinging sensation crept over my cheeks. "Yeah, well . . . it ended up being my sister's boyfriend, not a prowler. Plus, I didn't throw it all that well. I ended up just catching his arms."

Lucas nodded. "It's hard to learn how to throw. But I could teach you. I could show you what I learned about lassoing, too."

"You would?" Darby asked. Now she was the one with big, shining eyes.

"That would be stupendous!" Delaney said.

"Great!" Lucas said. "How about today? I mean . . . you know . . . if you can stick around longer." For some reason, he looked right at me as he said this.

"I . . . um . . . I guess we could," I said. "We have some time before Dad gets home."

Delaney nodded. "Yep. All we have to do later is return Ms. Woolcott's cake pan and fake baby."

"Great!" Lucas said, tossing the net onto a beanbag chair. "I'll go downstairs and get us some snacks. Be right back!"

"Thanks!" Delaney said. As soon as Lucas left she headed for a small trampoline in the corner and started jumping on it.

"Your face is still a little pink," Darby said to me.

"Huh?" I put my hand on my forehead.

"When you were giving the net to Lucas," she said. "Your cheeks turned the same color as that stomachache medicine Mom gives us."

"So? What are you saying?" I could feel my cheeks warming up again, so I looked down and pretended to be very interested in the robot dinosaur.

"Are you starting to like Lucas?"

"Oh, stop. Why would I like Lucas?" For some reason, the tingling in my face was getting worse.

"I know you've been mad at him because of the whole pageant thing," Darby said. "But you have to admit, Lucas has been nice to us lately. Don't you think?"

"I don't know. Has he?" I said. I glanced at Darby and saw she was grinning. It annoyed the heck out of me.

"Maybe . . . Lucas . . . likes . . . you," Delaney said, uttering one word per bounce.

I made a loud *ugh* sound and looked up at the ceiling. "That is the most preposterous thing I've ever heard."

Just then, Lucas burst into the room, carrying a tray. On top were a pile of cookies and four small boxes of chocolate milk. "Here you go," he said, setting it down on the Ping-Pong table. "If you want something else, let me know and I'll go grab it."

I squinted at him. "Lucas, how come you're being so nice to us?"

"What?" he asked, his eyebrows high with surprise.

Out of the corner of my eye, I could see Delaney stop bouncing and step down off the trampoline. Darby ducked her head as if embarrassed. But I kept my gaze on Lucas.

"I don't know," he said. "It's just . . . You guys never come over anymore. I never see anyone hardly. It stinks."

I cocked my head and stared at Lucas, pondering him. I thought hard about everything that had happened during the past few days — but also during the last year or so. And I thought about what Darby and Delaney had said before he came back with snacks.

Lucas was right. We didn't visit him any longer, and I wasn't exactly sure why.

And even though Lucas had every gadget, game, and piece of sports equipment ever invented, there was something he didn't have: siblings. I imagined that got pretty lonely. My sisters were not just family, they were also my best friends. So even though I didn't have a lot of cool, expensive stuff, I always had people around I could have fun with.

I noticed other things, too. Like that Lucas had eyes the same color blue as the field behind the stars on our flag. And they looked all gleamy whenever he was interested in something. In fact, there was something kind of noble about him. Not noble like an oppressive monarch, though. Noble like a decent, dignified citizen — like a young George Washington, with braces.

"Lucas, I'm sorry," I said.

He looked confused. "About what?"

"I'm sorry we haven't come over unless it was to accuse you of a crime or borrow equipment. And I'm sorry I've been kind of crabby. I guess I was just jealous."

"Jealous?" Again Lucas's eyebrows became high half circles. "Of my stuff?"

I shook my head. "Not your stuff. Although you do have cool things."

"Yep, you do," came Delaney's muffled voice from inside a space helmet.

"I was jealous because . . . because . . ." I stopped, swallowed, and closed my eyes. "Because you got cast as a Wise Man and I didn't," I finished real fast.

Someone was patting my back. I glanced behind me and saw Darby, looking proud.

"Aw, heck. I didn't even want to be a Wise Guy," Lucas said. "Neither did Adam or Tommy."

"You didn't?" I asked.

He shook his head. "Nope. We wanted to be the barn animals. We'd each been practicing making the sounds for over a week."

"Really?" I said. "Huh. Well, what do you know . . ." I started wandering around the room, tapping my finger against my chin.

"I know that look," Darby said.

"What look?" Lucas asked.

"She's getting a good idea," Delaney said. "Aren't you, Dawn?"

I smiled. "I think I am."

CHAPTER TWENTY-ONE

Glory Glory Hallelujah

Darby

Delaney, cut it out!" Dawn said in a loud whisper. "You're bouncing on my feet."

"Sorry," Delaney replied.

"*Shhh!*" I said.

We were backstage in the sanctuary, waiting for Reverend Hoffmeyer to give us the signal. And, as usual, Delaney couldn't keep still.

Lucas came over to us, grinning. He was wearing donkey ears and a brown robe with a tail, and his braces glistened like tinsel in the dim light. "This is going to be so cool," he said, looking at Dawn. "Thanks for figuring all this out."

"Shucks." Dawn looked down to where her sneakers

were poking out of the bottom of her robe. "I didn't do much, really."

All in all, Mrs. Higginbotham took it pretty well when Dawn told her at rehearsal that the pageant had recast itself. Mrs. Higginbotham just smiled a skinny-looking smile and said, "Very well. If there is no need for my input and guidance, then you may do the pageant yourselves."

"Wow, thanks, Mrs. Higginbotham!" Dawn said.

We started to walk away, but Mrs. Higginbotham kept on talking. "No need to worry yourself over my concerns." She raised her chin and stared at the ceiling. "It's not for nothing that I work hard for this church."

"You mean . . . you get paid?" Dawn asked.

"Indeed not." Mrs. Higginbotham just kept glancing upward. "I meant that I do it out of the kindness of my heart. And now this is the thanks I get."

Delaney nodded. "Huh. I never really considered this a thank-you to you, but I guess it is in a way. So you're welcome!"

"Especially if you don't get paid," Dawn said. "Now we can take it from here."

At that point, Mrs. Higginbotham rose from her seat

and said, "Come, Bertram. We aren't needed." She walked halfway down the aisle and then looked back. "Bertram?"

That's when Mr. Higginbotham stood and said, "Uh-uh. Still have to do my part," and headed toward the nook with the light board and sound equipment. As he passed me, he gave a little smile and nod.

Mrs. Higginbotham made a few sputtering noises, like Dad's van when it has trouble starting. Then she called out, "Fine. Good luck to you all," and disappeared through the door. I thought it was mighty nice of her. Maybe St. Nick had listened to my wish after all.

After she left, we practiced the play, with Dawn giving us directions. She wasn't as bossy as I thought she'd be, and I had to admit it was a much better show with the new casting. Lucas, Adam, and Tommy got to do the animal parts, and they were really good, too. It was clear they'd been practicing. The smaller kids got to be angels — which they were excited about because they could move and sway and didn't have to keep still. Lucy and Wilson were boyfriend and girlfriend again, so they stayed Mary and Joseph. And Dawn, Delaney, and I got to be the Three Wise People. Everything was just right.

Of course, I was still nervous. I'm a very shy person, and whenever I have to stand up in front of a bunch of people who are watching me, I feel a little like throwing up and a lot like running away and hiding.

So as we waited in the wings, my stomach felt like a ship in a storm, pitching and lurching inside me.

And then . . . I heard the signal.

"It's 'Hark, the Herald Angels Sing'!" I whisper-shouted. "After this, Reverend Hoffmeyer will announce us." I felt a little unsteady with that thunderstorm in my gut. I really hoped I could get through the show.

The song ended and there was a small rumbling sound as everyone sat back down. "And now," Reverend Hoffmeyer said, "we bring you the miracle of Christmas!"

Lucas, Tommy, and Adam took their places in the stable, and then Lucy walked out, holding the baby doll, with Wilson at her side. Both of them looked solemn yet serene, just like Dawn had told them to. After that, Dawn gestured to the little angels, who were already swaying backstage, and they headed out onto the stage. I could hear the people in the crowd go, "Aww."

Then it was our turn.

I had that balloon-y feeling in my chest — the one I get before hiccups — and my legs felt like noodles underneath my robe. I gulped a couple of times and made myself follow Dawn as she started doing her wise walk.

As we trudged toward the entrance to the stage, we passed Mr. Higginbotham in his corner working the lights and sound. He smiled and gave us a thumbs-up. For some reason, that made the squall inside my belly settle down a lot.

The audience was only partially illuminated, and I was trying not to look at them, but I could tell that everyone was smiling. I recognized Dad's shiny head as he stood off to the side with his camcorder.

We marched to the manger with our heads high and noble and one by one announced our gifts. I set down the cup that was supposed to be frankincense in front of Lucy, Wilson, and the baby doll in the manger, and then took my place next to Dawn, facing the audience.

I'm not sure if the crowd could hear my loud gasp or not. But suddenly I didn't have to pretend to behold a wondrous sight, because my eyes were witnessing an actual marvel.

Standing at the very back of the church were Mom, Lily, and Aunt Jane. I blinked a few times to make sure my eyes weren't playing a joke on me, but it was them, all right. They were still wearing their coats and they were smiling big smiles that shined in the dim light.

It took every bit of focus and energy for us to stay in our places, finish the play, and sing "Silent Night" with the audience. I was proud of Delaney for holding fairly still. She wiggled only slightly, and she did make a high-pitched noise, but I think only Dawn and I could hear it. And maybe any nearby dogs.

Finally, it was over and everyone clapped and clapped. We took our bows and bounded off the stage, racing over to Mom, Lily, and Aunt Jane.

"You made it!" exclaimed Delaney, who got there first.

"I'm so happy to see you!" I said, tossing my arms around Mom.

"How in the world did you get here?" asked Dawn, coming up behind me.

"It's a long story," Lily said. She and Mom looked at each other and shook their heads, as if they could hardly believe it themselves.

Just then, Mrs. Higginbotham walked up. She was

smiling at me, Dawn, and Delaney and clapping softly with her hands.

"I must say, you girls did a fine job," she said. "At the end of the day, we all want what's best for everyone, don't we?"

"Yes, we do," Delaney said. "And at the start of the day, too."

"Hello, Annie. So nice to see you," Mrs. Higginbotham greeted Mom. "Did you bring those cookies?"

Mom smiled really big. "No, I did not."

"Oh. Well . . . I see." Mrs. Higginbotham didn't seem to know what to say. "Excuse me. I have to help with refreshments. Enjoy your holiday!"

"You, too!"

As she disappeared into the milling-about crowd, we continued to swarm Mom, Lily, and Aunt Jane. "I still don't understand," Dawn said. "How did you guys get here?"

Aunt Jane chuckled. "Come on. I'll show you," she said, and gestured for us to follow her.

She started filling us in as we headed down the main corridor to the front doors of the church. Apparently, when Mom and Lily couldn't get on a plane, and all the rental cars were spoken for, Aunt Jane got an idea.

"I thought, well, what else can you get for a one-way trip somewhere?"

"A moving van?" I exclaimed as we headed out to the parking lot. Aunt Jane was motioning toward a yellow truck with EASY HAUL-EM written on the side that was parked along the curb. Probably because it didn't fit in a regular parking spot.

"Yep," Lily said. "That was our ride."

I turned to Aunt Jane. "But why did you come?"

"I couldn't let them drive that far by themselves," she said. "This way we split it up three ways so no one got too tired. Besides, how could I pass up an excuse to see my nieces?"

"Jane!" Dad pushed through the door to the church and jogged over to us. Then he and Aunt Jane did that thing they always do where they pretend to box each other and end up hugging. "What a nice surprise."

"Had to come. Sounds like I've been missing out on all kinds of shenanigans," Aunt Jane said. "And speaking of surprises, we have one for you."

Dad's brow lowered over his eyes. "You do?"

"Indeed we do. Take a look at this." Aunt Jane walked over to the moving van, unlocked it, and lifted the back door. In the faint glow of the parking lot light we could just make out a distinctive-looking shape under plastic wrap.

"A sofa?" Dad asked.

"A sofa!" Dawn, Delaney, and I exclaimed.

"We passed through Memphis on the way down," Lily said. "We were getting gas, and we saw this couch in the front window of a used furniture store. It looked like you."

"Bald on top?" Dad joked.

"No. Hip and cool — but, you know, not brand-new," Lily said.

Dad laughed. "That's so thoughtful. You guys didn't need to do that."

"Just consider it a big 'I'm sorry' from Quincy," Mom said.

Everyone chuckled at that.

I turned in a slow circle, scanning the happy faces of Dawn, Delaney, Dad, Aunt Jane, Mom, and Lily. Everywhere I turned there was someone I loved. It was complete and perfect.

I thought about the Joy and Peace I felt just seeing them and being with them. I thought about how we were willing to give up all our presents in order to be with Lily and Mom for Christmas. I thought about how all the presents that Lucas got didn't make him as happy as having friends to enjoy them with, and what Mr. Neighbor had said about our help being a gift.

And right then, I figured out what we should give Mom for Christmas.

CHAPTER TWENTY-TWO

Freedom Ring

Delaney

On Christmas Day I woke up before anyone else, as usual. At least, I thought I did.

I had so many happy thoughts and feelings hollering inside me, I couldn't sleep, and I planned to dance around in the yard with Quincy until I could be still.

I put on my shoes and my coat over my pajamas and went downstairs, keeping the lights off so that I didn't wake anyone. Aunt Jane was snoring on the couch, so I planned to take the back door. But when I headed into the kitchen, there was someone standing there.

I was so surprised, I almost let out an intolerable scream. I thought for sure it was a real prowler this time, or the bathroom ghost out for an early morning stroll.

But then I noticed the coffee cup in the figure's hand and the short hair sticking out in all directions. Mom.

"Did you girls do this?" she asked me. She gestured around the kitchen at the clean floor and empty sink and empty trash can.

I nodded. "It was supposed to be a surprise."

"It was." She smiled. "Did Aunt Jane help you?"

"No, we told her not to. It was our gift to you, so that meant we had to do it ourselves," I explained. "Although she did keep a lookout in case you woke up."

"You girls were probably up pretty late. I'll let poor Jane sleep in today."

I grinned and bounced. It was so nice to have Mom back where she belonged.

"Were you heading out to run around with Quincy?" she asked.

"Yep."

"When you're done, can you help me quietly make breakfast? It's going to be a big day. We'll want to fuel up before we open gifts."

Gifts! I'd been so happy about solving the Santa mystery and the pageant and Mom, Lily, and Aunt Jane showing up, I'd almost forgotten that I'd have presents to open.

"Sure!" I said.

I ran into the utility room and was just about to open the back door when an important thought came over me. I ran back to the kitchen, where Mom was pouring herself another cup of coffee.

I watched her as she added a teaspoon of sugar and stirred. My mom. She had fought through ice and snow to be here. She was like the U.S. Postal Service — only better.

"Hey, Mom?"

She paused in the middle of taking a sip and looked up at me. "Yes?"

"Thanks for being our mom."

Her smile widened and her eyes looked twinkly. "You're welcome. Thank you for being my thoughtful daughter."

"You're welcome," I said, and I twirled out onto the porch to get Quincy.

It was a historic Christmas. The family Christmas against which all others would be measured.

After everyone had woken up and eaten breakfast, and Dawn, Darby, and I were getting the kitchen back to its ultraclean, giftlike condition for Mom, there was a knock at the front door. I zoomed over to answer it.

Aunt Jane was sitting on the couch, drinking coffee. "Hmmm. I wonder who that could be?" she asked. The way she said it, kind of loud and obvious and with a wink in her voice, made me know something was up.

Before I could reach the door, it opened a little and Dad poked his head inside. "Ho ho ho!" he said. A Santa cap sat on top of his usual baseball cap. He struggled the rest of the way inside, trying not to bang his armload of wrapped presents against the doorframe.

"Dad!" Dawn cried, racing into the room. Darby came in behind her, both of them wide-eyed with surprise.

"What are you doing here?" I asked, twirling around him as he walked inside and sneaking looks to see which of the boxes he was holding had my name on it. "I thought we were going to your place this evening."

"Your mom and Aunt Jane invited me," he said.

"This way your celebration won't get divided up," Aunt Jane said. "We'll all be together for the present opening."

Dawn, Darby, and I cheered.

"Oh, good. Now we can start Christmas," Mom said, coming into the room. She was also holding a couple of wrapped gifts. The trip had put her behind on her wrapping, and she'd been back in her room getting caught up.

When Lily came out to greet Dad she was holding her cell phone and had a familiar dreamy look on her face.

"Talking with Alex?" Dad asked as he leaned down to hug and kiss her.

"Yes," she said with a shy smile.

"Tell him to get over here soon!" I said.

"He'll be here in a little while," she said. "No need to wait on him."

We turned the living room chairs to face the tree, and everyone gathered around to open presents. Dawn loved her White House model kit. Darby loved her Declaration of Independence puzzle. And I loved the historically accurate Civil War signal whistle that my sisters gave me. Mom loved the coupons we made for Cleaning Up Without Complaining, Quiet Time, and Breakfast in Bed That Isn't Burned. (I grabbed a pen and paper and quickly added one for No Whistle Blowing for Three Straight Hours.) Also, Dad loved the guitar-shaped pillow we got him and said it would look great on his new couch, and Lily said she adored her bracelet.

As Lily put on the bracelet and we all admired it, Dad stood up and said, "Well, I think it's my turn." He stepped through the front door and came back carrying a cage with a cloth cover over it.

"Delaney, this is for you," he said, setting it carefully on the floor. "She's not an exotic bird, but we hope you'll like her." He pulled the cover off the cage, and there sat an adorable bunny.

She was beautiful. Soft and smoky-colored, with big brown eyes and a wriggly nose, and a tuft of fur that stuck up at the top of her head. The minute I saw her I let out a squealing sound that made everyone cover their ears.

I knew she wouldn't ever talk, but she could bounce, and that was just as good. I loved her as soon as I saw her, and right away I named her Mynah.

"Thank you, Dad," I said, throwing my arms around him.

"Actually, the rabbit is from your mom," he said. "My present is that I'll be building her a hutch over here in the backyard today — with your help, of course."

"And mine," Aunt Jane volunteered.

Dawn got a portable microphone and speaker with volume control and Darby got a gift certificate to a trapeze class in Austin. They were both thrilled.

We gave Aunt Jane the Screaming Banana, and she loved it. She juggled it between her hands and laughed as it screeched and hollered.

Soon we were all bouncing happily like Mynah. Everywhere I turned there was something to make me smile. My cute rabbit. My dog sniffing my cute rabbit. Darby doing her puzzle. Dawn reciting the Gettysburg Address on her microphone (with the speaker turned down low). Mom relaxing with a book Lily gave her. Lily telling Dad about her trip to Boston. Dad showing me and Aunt Jane the plans for the hutch.

Then the doorbell rang and Lily opened it to find Mr. and Mrs. Neighbor holding a pan of gingerbread.

"Just a little something to say thank you for your help," Mrs. Neighbor said.

They even brought the St. Nick figurine with them to show us that he'd been mended. He was still a little discolored in places, but strangely enough, a tiny dent in his forehead made him look less frown-y.

No sooner had Mom invited them inside and asked to hear firsthand about the Santa-napping raccoon fiasco, the doorbell rang again. This time it was Ms. Woolcott carrying a freshly baked king cake, also as a thank-you — but also as an apology for calling the cops on us.

I know Ms. Woolcott and the Neighbors were just saying thank you, but it was Christmas, so we felt kind of funny getting gifts from people and not giving anything in return. So Dawn, Darby, and I presented the Neighbors with the bird feeder Dawn had bought, to thank them for all the hot chocolates and gingerbread and sprinkler fun. And we gave Ms. Woolcott the cookie cutter set that Darby had bought, to thank her for the toffee and king cake and freshly cut flowers she shares with us in the springtime. (But also, secretly, as a sorry for thinking she could have been the Santa-napper.)

Now our group was even bigger and cozier than before. It felt like our happiness was spreading outward.

But there was still one more astonishing turn of events to go. The best surprise of all.

The doorbell rang and I answered since I was closest. Out on the porch stood Alex. He seemed a little nervous — maybe because he'd been attacked with a net and marshmallows on that exact spot two nights before. "Hi there," he said.

Lily came up behind me. "You're here!" she said in that extra-musical tone of voice she uses with him.

"You're back," he said, with that big smile he uses only on Lily. "I got here as soon as I could."

She stepped forward and gave him a smooch, and I let out a high-pitched noise. I was so happy to see them back together.

"I have your present," Alex said to Lily. "I want to give it to you as soon as possible."

"Come on in," Lily said. She stepped aside, and I pulled the door wide so he could enter.

"Alex! Alex! Hey, everyone, it's Alex!" I shouted over the hubbub in the living room.

Everyone said "Hi" and "Welcome" and "Merry Christmas" as he stepped through the doorway. Dawn and Darby ran over to greet him.

"Alex came to give Lily her present," I announced. Alex just stood there, smiling, but otherwise not doing a thing. I then noticed that he wasn't carrying a gift. "Do you need to go to your car and get it?"

"No. I have it," he said. He turned toward Lily, opened his mouth, closed it, then turned and looked at all the people staring at them. He seemed surprised to see everyone — especially the neighbors.

"You can go ahead and give it to her," Dawn prodded.

"There's no hurry," Lily said. She was staring at Alex, and her forehead had three faint squiggles on it. I could tell she was concerned by his odd behavior. Little did she know he'd been acting kooky for days.

"It's okay," he said with a quick laugh. "It's just . . . now? Here? In front of everyone?"

"Yes. We already opened gifts," Dawn said.

"And we were about to have dessert," Darby said.

"And I want to see what you got her," I added.

Lily gave me an eye-rolly look. "Don't listen to them," she said to Alex. "It can wait till later."

Alex raked his fingers through his hair and blew out his breath. "No, I'm going to. I've been worrying about this for a while now, and I should just go for it."

His face and voice were suddenly serious-sounding. Dawn, Darby, and I exchanged worried looks.

Alex grabbed Lily's left hand and held it in both of his. "I was going to write you a poem, but nothing sounded right. I even thought about a greeting card, but that was an even worse idea. So, I just decided to let the action speak for itself." He took a deep breath and got down on one knee. Then he reached into his jacket pocket and pulled out a small black box with a tiny silver bow on top and handed it to Lily.

Lily gasped and put her hands over her mouth.

"Merry Christmas, Lily. Will you marry me?"

It was the most beautiful and magical of all our Christmas miracles. The only downside was that no one actually heard her say yes because I let out one of my intolerable screams.

But then they were kissing, so it was obvious she had accepted his proposal. And then everyone was hugging and crying and laughing and bouncing and shrieking with joy. I even did cartwheels on the dining room rug. I was so happy, I felt like I could zoom to the moon with one jump. People really should have fireworks handy for such occasions, because the moment deserved to be celebrated in a big, loud, sparkling way.

Once we'd all settled down, Alex sat on the couch next to Lily and put the ring on her finger. We all gathered around to admire it. The ring had one small diamond with two dark blue sapphires, Lily's birthstone, on either side of it. It was beautiful without being big and showy — perfect for Lily.

Next they answered a lot of questions about when the wedding would happen (they didn't know — not until they were done with school), whether Lily would still go to graduate school (of course), and whether she had known this was coming (no). Alex explained that he'd been really nervous leading up to this moment, made worse by the suspense of not knowing when Lily would be back — and even more worse by his fear that we'd seen him coming out of the jewelry store on the day he bought the ring.

"Oh! Is that why you were acting so wackadoo?" Dawn asked.

Alex laughed. "I guess I was acting weird. Sorry about that."

"I have an important question," Aunt Jane said. She stood behind the couch with her left hand on his right shoulder and a serious look on her face. "Alex, are you absolutely certain you want to be part of this crazy family?"

"And this extended neighborhood family?" Mr. Neighbor added.

Alex looked around at all of us and his smile grew wider. "Yes. I'm absolutely certain."

"Then we accept your proposal," Aunt Jane said. "I pronounce this engagement official!"

We laughed and the celebrating started all over again.

It was hard to believe that this started out as the worst Christmas ever. But once we started focusing on what mattered, instead of what we wanted, it ended up being the best.

I guess with all the screaming and running around, we didn't exactly help with peace on earth. But we did learn more about spreading goodwill to family, friends, neighbors, pets, and even sneaky raccoons with a sweet tooth. We also got the most wonderful gifts ever. I don't mean the books, games, puzzles, or even Mynah. I mean that we got a soon-to-be brother-in-law, a surprise visit from Aunt Jane, and a little bit of wisdom.

And hopefully, if we're good about listening and learning, we'll just keep on getting wiser.

ACKNOWLEDGMENTS

So many people have assisted me, encouraged me, and made me wiser.

Deepest gratitude goes to Erin Black. Thank you for loving these girls and their wackadoo ways.

Forever thanks goes to Erin Murphy for loving my wackadoo ways.

Thank you, David Levithan, Charisse Meloto, Jeremy West, Yaffa Jaskoll, Beka Wallin, Caitlin Mahon, Lizette Serrano, Emily Heddleson, Antonio Gonzalez, and the rest of the Scholastic team.

Thank you, Becka Oliver, for supporting this project. I couldn't have done it without you.

Thank you to the EMLA Gangos for the cheers, laughter, and wonderful reads that inspire.

Thank you to my Texas-based creative tribe — especially the Austin SCBWI and Writers' League of Texas. Of this group, special thanks go to Noelle O'Donnell, Clare Dunkle, Varian Johnson, Cynthia Leitich Smith, Greg Leitich Smith, Carol Dawson, Nichole Chagnon, Sarah Bird, Nikki Loftin, Alex Loucel, April Lurie, Margo Rabb, Clay Smith, Carlotta Stankiewicz, Cynthia Levinson, Kari Ann Holt, Owen Egerton, Jodi Egerton, Arden, and Oscar. You have all helped me in ways that you may or may not know. I'm lucky to be part of this community.

Thank you, Johnson City, Texas. Wandering your roads, taking in your history, and meeting your residents is the best of all inspiration.

And thank you to my nearest and dearest: my children, Owen, Sage, Renee, and Fletcher; my parents, Jim and Esther Ford; and my sister, Amanda Ford. Extra thanks to my little brother, Jason Ford, who helped me with research.

With every one of my ventures, I am aided and encouraged by my husband and best friend, Chris Barton. Thank you, love of mine. Being with you is truly a gift.

ABOUT THE AUTHOR

Like the Brewster triplets, **Jennifer Ziegler** is a native Texan and a lover of family, history, barbecue, and loyal dogs. Although she only has one sister, she does know what it is like to have four kids living in the same house. She is the author of *Revenge of the Flower Girls*, as well as books for older readers, including *Sass & Serendipity* and *How Not to Be Popular*. Jennifer lives in Austin, Texas, with her husband, author Chris Barton, and their four children.